Thumbprint Mysteries

DEAD MAN RIDING

BY

PATRICIA MATTHEWS

CONTEMPORARY BOOKS

a division of NTC/CONTEMPORARY PUBLISHING GROUP
Lincolnwood, Illinois USA

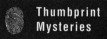

Thumbprint
Mysteries

MORE THUMBPRINT MYSTERIES

by Patricia Matthews:

The Secret of Secco Canyon
Death in the Desert

This is a work of fiction. The characters, incidents, and dialogues are products of the author's imagination and are not to be construed as real. Any resemblance to actual events or persons, living or dead, is entirely coincidental.

Cover Illustration: Matt Zumbo

ISBN: 0-8092-0607-2

Published by Contemporary Books,
a division of NTC/Contemporary Publishing Group, Inc.,
4255 West Touhy Avenue,
Lincolnwood (Chicago), Illinois 60646-1975 U.S.A.
Manufactured in the United States of America.

890 QB 0 9 8 7 6 5 4 3 2 1

CHAPTER 1

The Prescott Rodeo, billed as "The Oldest Rodeo in the World," was in full swing. The aging stadium held an enthusiastic crowd that cheered loudly and applauded after every event.

Over the loudspeaker, the announcer's voice could be heard in every corner of the stadium. "Now coming out of chute number three, Rob Hardesty, riding Old Thunder. Give him a big hand, folks!"

Rob Harding, sitting tensely on the bunched back of the quivering bronc, took a deep breath. He still felt strange hearing himself referred to by another name. It was one of the most difficult things about working undercover. Then the chute opened; now he had no time to think of anything except staying on the back of this angry mass of muscle called a horse.

The crowd applauded lustily as the gate to chute number three swung wide. Old Thunder boiled out of the chute almost before it was open. Dust rose up in clouds under the horse's pounding hooves as he bucked wildly.

Lowering his head, the animal flung his rear hooves into the air. Rob clamped his legs as tightly as he could around the trunk of the bucking horse. Under rodeo rules he wasn't allowed to touch the saddle horn. Also, to score points, a rider is supposed to spur his horse with each buck. A ride is limited to eight seconds, and horses buck from eight to thirteen times during that time. Points are awarded for the length of each slash of the spurs. The spurs are blunted so the animal will not be harmed.

Rob knew that he was slowly losing his grip. Every time Old Thunder bucked, Rob's legs and thighs slipped a little. He desperately tried to rake his spurs along the animal's flanks. But it was not to be. Old Thunder launched himself skyward again. It seemed to Rob that the animal would never come down. Then the horse landed with all four feet, and Rob felt the jar all the way up to the top of his head. The instant Old Thunder's hooves hit the dirt, the horse bucked again, twisting first to one side, then to the other.

Rob lost it. He flew out of the saddle like a missile being launched, landing hard on his back. He struggled to maintain consciousness. As he attempted to peer from dust filled eyes, he heard an alarmed roar from the crowd.

He managed to raise his head, to see Old Thunder charging right at him! The horse, eyes wild, reared back, raising both front legs. The hooves, Rob knew, were shod. If the metal horseshoes struck him in the face or head, it could kill him!

He gathered his strength and rolled twice. The horse's hooves slashed down, striking the ground only inches from his head. Dust flew up and into Rob's eyes. He blinked rapidly, trying to clear his vision.

To his surprise he heard shouts of laughter from the crowd. Were they laughing at him? They couldn't be that unkind!

He finally managed to raise himself on one elbow and saw what had drawn the laughter from the audience.

It was Elmo, the rodeo clown. Elmo wore loose, short-legged trousers held up by flaming red suspenders. He also wore a long-sleeved man's undershirt. On his head was a tiny Stetson, held in place by a rubber band under his chin. His face was painted white, except for his mouth and nose. They were painted a deep red. Orange hair sprouted from under the tiny hat.

He had a bullfighter's red cape in his hands, which he waved in front of Old Thunder. The horse snorted, pawing the ground; but his attention was drawn away from Rob. Elmo advanced on the animal, waving the red cape. Old Thunder snorted in fear and backed away. Then he turned and galloped toward the arena fence. There, the pickup men rode up to Old Thunder and herded him out of the arena.

Two men were running toward Rob, who was now struggling to sit up. They caught him by the arms and helped him to stand.

The crowd went wild, shouting its approval of Elmo. The clown faced the stands and bowed. Holding the red cape before his face, he peered around the edge of it shyly. The crowd roared with laughter.

One of the men holding Rob said, "You okay, Hardesty?"

"Yeah, I'm fine, physically, but my pride is a little bruised."

"No need, Hardesty," the second man said. "Heck, I don't think any man could have ridden Old Thunder the way he was today. I don't know what put a burr under his saddle. I've seen him in several rodeos the last two years. I've never seen him this wild."

"Can you make it by yourself, Hardesty?" the first man asked.

"Oh, sure. Thanks, guys."

The two men walked back toward the chutes. Rob stood for a moment. Then he removed his gloves and used them to beat the dust from his clothes.

He walked over to pick up his Stetson and whacked it against his leg a few times to get some of the dust off. Then he went over to where Elmo, the clown, was standing as he waited near the chutes for the next event to begin. Rob wasn't sure he would recognize the clown in his normal clothes and without makeup. He'd never seen Elmo as himself. In the rodeo program Elmo's real name was listed as Jack Babcock.

Rob said, "Thanks, Elmo, for saving my bacon. Old Thunder could have stomped my face in if you hadn't drawn him off."

Elmo turned his gray eyes on Rob. The painted rings around his eyes gave him the look of a raccoon. His painted lips drew back in a grin. He said, "Think nothing of it . . . Hardesty, is it?"

Rob nodded, "Yeah. Rob Hardesty."

Elmo nodded. "Anyway, Hardesty, it's all in a day's work. I've seen that horse work before. He's a rough ride, but I've never seen him like this. He went crazy there for a bit."

"You never know with horses," Rob said with a shrug. "They're like people, I guess. We all have our bad days. Anyway, thanks again."

He held out his hand. Elmo took it. His grip was strong. With all the makeup it was hard to tell, but Rob judged the man to be in his late forties or early fifties.

Rob nodded and strolled toward the chutes. To his surprise he noticed that he was limping slightly and there was a growing soreness in his left knee. He must have twisted it in falling. Now he noticed other aches. He was going to be sore and black and blue all over by tomorrow. He was glad that he wasn't entered in any more events today.

He walked on more slowly. A good-looking man, just past thirty, Rob was tall and well-built. The coppery tint of his skin showed his Navajo blood. His eyes were dark gray and his hair was black, worn long. He had a strong face with a prominent nose and a good mouth.

As he went through the gate leading out of the arena, he saw another rodeo rider that he knew slightly. The rider was leaning against the side of a chute. He, like Rob, was wearing faded jeans, heavy chaps, and cowboy boots with dulled spurs. The Stetson set back on his head was old and black with sweat stains.

He said, "Tough luck, Rob. You gave Old Thunder a good ride there for a bit."

Rob grunted. "Yeah. For two hops and a skip."

The other man grinned. "New at this, ain't you?"

"This is my first year on the circuit, yeah."

The other man nodded. "Figured. Wait until you've been at it as long as I have. You'll learn that your luck can turn sour at any time. This just wasn't your day."

Rob gave a short laugh. "You can say that again."

He walked on as the announcer blared over the loudspeakers, "Rob Hardesty scored a 62. Better luck next time, Rob. Next out of chute number four is Jeff Martin, riding Cyclone!"

62! A terrible score. To have any chance at prize money a bronc rider had to score at least 80.

Rob leaned against the railing and watched as the gate swung open. The horse named Cyclone exploded out of the gate. *My horse should have been named Cyclone,* Rob thought. *He certainly twisted enough and rose high enough to be a cyclone.*

Cyclone bucked and twisted across the arena. Dust puffed up from beneath the animal's pounding hooves. The rider stuck with him. He raked the horse's flanks with his spurs, strokes that extended from the horse's shoulders to his flanks. He remained in the saddle the full eight seconds required. Then he dismounted on his own as the audience cheered loudly. The rider bowed to the crowd, then strutted back toward the chutes. Two men on horseback, the pickup men, crowded the still-bucking horse toward the gate. Finally they got him pinned against the railing. One cowboy seized the reins as they led the now docile animal out of the arena.

It was the last day of the rodeo, and Rob had given two decent rides before today. Yet he knew that his name would be far down the list when the results were posted.

It's a good thing I don't rodeo for a living, Rob thought sourly. It was also a good thing that his boss, Stanley Morgan, had paid the entry fee. Rob certainly couldn't have paid it out of any prize money.

He jumped as a voice spoke behind him: "You're Rob Hardesty, aren't you?"

"Yes, I am," Rob replied. He had early learned that it was best to use a cover name close to his own. Otherwise, he might not react quickly enough when spoken to.

The man facing him was tall and weathered. He was wearing a cowman's working clothes. His face was leathery from long exposure to the hot sun of Arizona. His faded blue eyes regarded Rob curiously. "I'm Jonas Greene."

He held out a hand and Rob shook it.

Jonas said, "I saw you ride the last couple of days. You're pretty good, Hardesty."

Rob laughed shortly. "You saw me today, on Old Thunder?" Jonas nodded with a faint smile. "And you can still say I'm a good rider?"

Jonas shrugged. "Anybody can have a bad day. Or a bad horse. I also saw your ride yesterday, not bad. Are you rodeoing for a living?"

Rob laughed again. "I had thought of it, but after what's happened here I'm about to change my mind."

"But you know horses, that's plain to see."

Rob said, "Well, I've been around horses a lot. For the past couple of years I've been a working cowhand, but that can be hard work, as I'm sure you know. I thought rodeoing might be a little easier." He laughed shortly. "I'm learning just how wrong I was!"

"That's what I wanted to talk to you about, Rob," Jonas said. "I own a spread over in Chino Valley. It's mostly stocked with cattle, but the cattle business isn't what it once was. So for the past two years, I've been turning more and more to horses. Stock horses, rodeo horses, I'm even thinking of raising a few racehorses."

"Racehorses?" Rob asked. "That's a pretty risky business, isn't it?"

Jonas nodded. "You're right, of course. But I'm just getting my toes wet, so to speak. I only have a half dozen horses that are possible racers. On the other hand, I have over two hundred head of horses altogether. That's what I wanted to speak to you about."

Rob's interest picked up. Maybe working the rodeo here was going to pay off after all. "You wanted to speak to me? About your horses?"

"Yeah. I need a good man to break them," Jonas said.

"Someone to make good cow horses out of most, and turn some into rodeo stock."

"I know nothing about racehorses," Rob said quickly.

"Didn't expect you would. I've hired a trainer for that, an old-timer with a good reputation."

Rob felt a surge of satisfaction, yet he didn't want to appear too eager. He said slowly, "I don't know if I've given the rodeo circuit a good shot yet."

"You said a moment ago that you were on the verge of giving it up," Jonas said. "It's a rough life, Rob. I've seen men who were good cowhands stick with the dream of getting first-prize money at the next rodeo, and the next. They stick with it until they are crippled or their kidneys are ruined by the constant pounding. Often they become hopeless drunks and bums. You don't want that for yourself, do you?"

"You're right, Mr. Greene, I don't," Rob said. "You've got yourself a horse wrangler. I just hope you won't be too disappointed."

"I'm sure I won't be."

They shook hands on the bargain. Then Jonas gave Rob directions on how to get to his ranch. He said, "I'll expect you tomorrow, Rob."

Rob watched the rancher walk away. He was elated. The first step in his newest investigation had been taken. He hadn't even had to approach a rancher looking for a job. Rob faced about and leaned on the railing again. He stared out at the activity in the arena without really seeing it.

*   *   *

Rob worked for the Governor's Task Force on Crime. This task force was set up to investigate special crimes. These were crimes that were difficult for other Arizona law officers to handle.

There were several reasons for this. Sometimes it was hard to decide to which jurisdiction the crime belonged. Other times, a task force was best equipped to investigate the matter. Generally, the task force became involved when undercover investigators were called for.

Rob had served several years in the Army. Most of his time in the Army had been with the Military Police. After he left the Army he had learned about the task force, which had just been formed. He had joined over a year ago. Rob's first case had involved the theft of Native American artifacts. This would be his second case.

Stanley Morgan, Rob's superior, was a short man in his fifties. He had blunt features with steely gray eyes and a snub nose. He seemed to have more energy than any man Rob had ever known. He was fiercely loyal to his investigators.

On that day three weeks ago Morgan had said, "I have a new assignment for you, Rob. You've had experience as a cowhand. And I understand you're good with horses."

Rob said, "Well, I don't know about being good, but I've been around horses, yeah."

"I've had a number of calls recently from ranchers in the northern part of the state," Morgan said. "It seems that cattle rustling is becoming a popular crime again. Shades of the days of the Old West!"

Rob said, "I don't think it's ever stopped. Ranchers are always losing a few head to rustlers."

"A few head, yes," Morgan said. "But it seems that it's more than just a few head of late. Some of the big ranchers have told me they're losing stock by the hundreds. Not only cattle, but some are losing horses as well."

"I can understand that," Rob said. "These days, horses are more valuable than cattle. The prices are up for riding horses, rodeo stock, as well as horses for working cattle.

How are the rustlers moving what they steal?"

Morgan said, "That hasn't been established yet. The ranchers who have contacted me seem puzzled."

"They're probably using cattle trucks," Rob said.

"That will be the first thing you need to find out, Rob. I have a new identity made up for you. Driver's license, Social Security number, and credit card. All made out in the name of Rob Hardesty."

Rob made a face. "Do we have to do that? Rob Hardesty! You know, I wake up at night, and it sometimes takes me a few minutes to recall what name I'm using."

Morgan laughed. "That's undercover for you. If you went by your real name and for some reason someone wanted to check, your cover would be blown."

"Okay, I'll get on it," Rob said with a sigh. "I think the best way to work it is for me to hit a few rodeos, as a bronc rider. My story can be that I want to get out of the circuit. Or, that I need to make some money working to fund my rodeoing habit."

Morgan nodded. "Sounds like a plan to me. Have you ridden broncs?"

Rob shook his head. "I'll need some training."

Morgan nodded. "Right. I'll get you the best."

He stood and held out his hand. "Good luck, Rob."

Rob smiled and shook Morgan's hand. "Thanks. That's something that I won't turn down."

CHAPTER
2

The rodeo people had a custom. After the last event of the day, many of them would gather in one of the larger horse barns. It was a relaxed time. They smoked and drank, but mostly they swapped tall tales.

Rob had come to enjoy these times. He loved to listen to the rodeo performers swap stories. He understood that many of the stories were exaggerations or outright lies. Still, they were fun to listen to. Now that he had made the first important step in his investigation, he could relax a little.

When he entered the barn, Rob saw a large group of people. They were gathered around the rodeo clown who had saved him from the slashing hooves of Old Thunder. Elmo still wore his makeup, but he had taken off his shirt and tiny hat. Although Elmo had a mat of gray hairs on his chest, he was lean and well-muscled. Rob thought the man was in good physical shape for someone of his apparent age.

Elmo was smoking a large cigar and sipping a bottle of beer. He was just finishing up a yarn when Rob sat down on a bale of hay close by.

Elmo spotted him and raised a hand. "Good thing for you, lad, that I just happened to be in the arena when that bronc tossed you on your butt."

Rob nodded. "I know, Elmo. You saved me from losing my good looks to that bronc. Thanks again."

"Don't mention it. Glad I was on deck when it happened."

One of the bull riders asked, "Hey, who's the best bull fighter ever?"

"Wick Peth, no question," Elmo said instantly.

Rob had learned that the clowns who lured the bulls away from the thrown bull riders were called bull fighters.

A woman said, "Some say that guy who became an actor in Western movies, Slim Pickens, was the best."

Elmo shrugged. "Different folks, different strokes. Old Slim was good, no question. But in my opinion none could top Wick. Ask any bull rider. I saw Wick break his fist once on a bull's nose. Wick's been known to travel miles out of his way to drop in on a sick bull rider.

"Hell, I recollect I was at the Snake River Stampede one time," Elmo went on. "I wasn't working that day, just watching. A bull rider was on a mean old bull and he got his hand hung up with the rope. He'd have been killed if Wick hadn't jumped in. Wick jumped astraddle that bull's neck and freed the rider's hand from the rope. Then he jumped off the bull and began slapping the bull's nose. This drew the bull far enough away for the pickup team to come in and get the rider."

Elmo laughed heartily. "Never seen nothing like that since then."

Another man said, "Yeah, I was there that day. I saw that. I was just a kid. My daddy, he took me to see the Stampede."

"I just remembered something else about Wick Peth," Elmo said with a smile. "Back in 1954 Wick was working a rodeo and couldn't find his clown pants. It was only a couple of minutes until time to go into the arena. So Wick borrowed a pair of pants from another clown. The trouble was, the other clown was much shorter than Wick, and the pants were too tight in the crotch. So Wick just cut out the crotch. That was the first time the short bull-fighting skirt was used, the skirt that the rodeo clowns wear in bull fighting today."

Everyone laughed at the story. Rob sat on, listening, as the talk moved on to other phases of rodeo lore. Their talk always fascinated him.

He had learned a great deal about rodeo people during his time on the circuit. To outsiders the rodeo often seemed like a secret fraternity. Rodeo people had their own rules, dress, and conduct.

Their moral code, often called "the cowboy code," was powerful. Rodeo performers seldom committed crimes, and they were extremely loyal to their own. Rob had been surprised to learn that they were always willing to perform for charity. Most of them contributed to a variety of worthy causes. Rob felt that a man or woman could follow the rodeo circuit and be proud to be a part of it.

The tale-spinning slowly came to a close. One by one, the men drifted off. When Rob left to drive to the motel where he was staying, Elmo was one of the few left.

*   *   *

Early the next morning Rob checked out of the motel and drove his pickup north out of Prescott into the Chino Valley. The town of Chino was only a short drive from Prescott, but the Greene Ranch was several miles farther on.

The day was heating up rapidly. A few clouds drifted across the deep blue of the sky like billowing ship's sails. The air smelled of sage and pine trees.

Following Greene's directions, Rob turned off the highway onto a gravel road heading west. The land through which he was driving was all ranch land. Houses were few and far between. The land was mostly flat, and at this time of year the grass was yellow or brown. Cattle grazed placidly in the fenced pastures on each side of the road. Far to the west, mountains rose jaggedly.

There was almost no traffic on the road. About halfway to the ranch, Rob came upon a semi-truck parked by the side of the road. It was a cattle truck, an eighteen-wheeler. The slatted bed of the truck was empty.

Rob saw no one around the truck. He pulled in behind it. When he shut off the motor, he could hear the sound of country-western music coming from the truck cab. He remembered his remark to Stanley Morgan, that the stock being stolen were probably transported by truck. With that in mind, he got out of the pickup and approached the truck cab warily.

Before he reached it, the door on the driver's side swung open. Rob knew that his arrival had been noticed in the big side view mirror.

The man who got out of the cab was a big man. When he stepped down to the ground, he towered at least six feet four. He was in his late forties, Rob judged, with a craggy face and flat gray eyes. The eyes were cold and unfriendly. He wore a baseball cap on his head with the brim turned to the back.

Rob said, "Having trouble here? Can I be of any help?"

The man's cold eyes moved to Rob's face. "Some engine trouble. I've called on my cell phone. A mechanic from Prescott is on his way."

"I'm Rob Hardesty," Rob said, holding out his hand.

The man shook it. "Troy Simms. Thanks for stopping and offering your help. Most people wouldn't have."

Rob grinned. "I've been stuck out in the middle of nowhere myself a time or two. Those times I wished some Good Samaritan would come along. Actually, I guess you couldn't really call this the middle of nowhere." He glanced at the empty, slat-sided truck bed. "There are ranch houses every few miles. You out here to pick up a load of cattle?"

Simms's cold eyes narrowed with suspicion. He took his time about replying. "You in the cattle business, Hardesty?"

Rob laughed. "I work on ranches, work with horses. That puts me around cattle, but I'd hardly call it the cattle business."

Simms was now gazing past Rob. His voice lightened with relief as he said, "That'll be my mechanic now."

Rob looked around. A dust cloud rose in the air a half mile down the road, created by a tow truck.

He looked again at Simms. "I hope it's nothing he can't fix."

Simms shrugged. "I'm sure he can have it running again in no time. Thanks again for offering help, Hardesty."

"You're welcome, I'm sure." Rob lifted a hand. "See you around sometime, Simms."

It wasn't until Rob was in his pickup and driving away that he realized Simms hadn't answered his question. He had neither confirmed nor denied that he was picking up a load of cattle. But if he was involved in hauling stolen cattle, he wouldn't be doing it in broad daylight, would he?

Two miles down the road, Rob saw the sign he'd been waiting for. There was a wooden gate with an arched frame overhead spelling out Greene Ranch.

Rob stopped the pickup and got out to open the gate; then he drove through and parked again to close it. He drove on, rattling over a cattle guard. The road here was dirt, not gravel, but it had been graded recently. He continued on, leaving a rooster tail of dust behind.

A mile farther on, he crested a small rise and saw a green valley below with a stream running through it. There was a cluster of out-buildings, and the main ranch house was shaded by huge oak trees growing on all sides. The main house was wood, painted a dark gray to blend in with the trees surrounding it.

Rob could see cattle grazing on the slopes and the bottom of the valley. In one fenced pasture, he saw some grazing horses. One long-legged colt frisked around a mature mare that Rob judged to be its mother.

Rob smiled to himself as he drove on. It was a pleasing sight; he was sure that he would like his job here. He had certainly liked Jonas Greene the one time he had met the man. Rob often thought that it would be nice to settle down on a place like this with a year-round job. It would be a pleasant, relaxed existence.

He laughed aloud, amused at himself. He knew that he would miss the excitement of working undercover. It was challenging work. There was nothing quite like the feeling of completing an assignment successfully. He even liked the occasional danger. On his last case, working on a ranch much like this one, he had come very close to getting killed.

Perhaps someday he would leave the task force and find a permanent job on a place like this. But not just yet. Not until it wasn't as exciting.

When Rob reached the main house, he parked and shut off the motor. As he got out, he admired the flower beds along the front porch, which were colorful with many blossoms.

He lifted his face to the sun as he took in the familiar smells of a working ranch. Manure, fresh hay, the sweat– of horses, plus the scent of the flowers before him. He knew that some of the odors he only imagined. Yet he knew that they were there.

As he started toward the house, the front door opened, and Jonas Greene emerged. He wore a welcoming smile as he came down the steps toward Rob. Jonas held out his hand. "Good morning, Rob. Welcome to Greene Ranch." He laughed. "My wife, Marge, said we should name it Greene Rancho. But I thought that was a little much."

As they shook hands, a young boy came through the open door. Rob judged him to be around seven. He had Jonas's blue eyes and much the same features as the older man. He was sturdy, and he walked with a swagger. The thumbs of his small hands were hooked into his belt. Rob smiled as he took in the sharp-toed cowboy boots and the too-large Stetson perched on the child's head. As he stopped beside Jonas, the boy removed the Stetson and scratched his nose.

Jonas beamed at the boy and tousled his mop of brown hair. "This is my son, Alan. Meet Rob Hardesty, the rodeo bronc rider I told you about, boy."

The boy's face lit up. "I'm going to be a rodeo rider when I grow up!"

Jonas laughed fondly. "He was born to rodeo, this one. When he was only three years old, he pestered me until I put him on a calf. I ran alongside the calf, holding onto his belt so he wouldn't fall off."

"I never fell off once," Alan said proudly.

"Whoa now, son! Let's not exaggerate. You fell off a number of times."

"Not since I was five, Daddy," the boy said with a pout.

Jonas turned to Rob. "How about I show you around the place, Rob?"

"That would be great," Rob said.

They started toward the corrals and stock barn, Alan skipping on ahead.

"Got married late in life." Jonas sounded faintly embarrassed. "That's why the boy's young as he is, and I'm longer in the tooth than most first-time fathers. Wife's some years younger than me too."

Rob could think of nothing to say to that.

Jonas continued, "Up until about eight years ago, I was in no position to get married. I was rodeoing across the West, lucky to earn enough in prize money to eat. Many's the time I slept in empty horse stalls. All I had was an old pickup and a horse trailer. It was sure as hell no life for a woman. I saw many a rodeo bum drag a woman around with him. The better-off ones had house trailers, but even then it's no life for a woman. After fifteen years of that I was about to quit, like you yesterday. Then I got better or lucky, I don't know which. I began to take a few purses."

Rob nodded. "The little time I've been rodeoing I've learned just how rough it can be."

"After I won a few large purses, I began looking for some property to buy," Jonas continued. "Ten years ago I found this place on sale, cheap. I bought it and began putting money into it. A year later I met Marge. I proposed, and we got married. Then Alan came along, and that was it for me. I quit rodeoing and settled down here. It's been rough too, but I'm still hanging in there."

Rob said, "I understand that cattle ranching is suffering these days."

They had reached the corral now, which held a half-dozen horses. They leaned on the corral fence, looking in.

"You got that right. What with falling prices and so forth, raising cattle isn't what it once was," Jonas said. "But as I mentioned yesterday, I'm leaning more and more toward raising rodeo stock. Bucking horses, saddle horses, calves for roping, even bulls."

Rob was looking at Alan. The boy was between the two men, his head poked through two lower rails. He was staring in fascination at the horses milling in the corral. Rob had been an only child and something of a loner. He knew very little about children of Alan's age, and he was wary around them.

Jonas evidently caught the direction of Rob's glance. He laughed. "I guess Alan's going to be doing the rodeoing in this family from now on. Maybe you can teach him a thing or two about bronc riding."

"I don't know," Rob said doubtfully. "I've had little experience around kids . . ."

Jonas continued as though Rob hadn't spoken. "We thought to discourage the boy, but since he seems so determined we decided to go with the flow. Did you know that they now have schools that teach people how to become rodeo performers?"

"Yes, I've run into several performers on the circuit who started in rodeo schools."

"I don't want that for Alan," Jonas said. He reached down to squeeze the boy's shoulder. Alan pulled away, moving a few feet down the railing. Jonas laughed and continued, "If he's going into rodeoing, he should do it the hard way. Rodeo's a hard life, and he'll need to be tough to survive. So will you give him a few pointers?"

Rob still had reservations, but he said, "I'll do what I can. But I don't know if I'm a good teacher. I'm curious, Mr. Greene. . . . You're an old-time rodeo hand. Why don't you teach him?"

"Jonas, please, Rob." Jonas shook his head. "I was a bull rider and a sometime calf roper. All rough stock events, as opposed to timed events, like bronc riding." He laughed with some embarrassment. "I was never very good on a horse."

He laughed again as Rob looked at him in astonishment. "I know, I know. A rancher who isn't good with a horse. A laugh, huh? I'm strictly a pickup rancher. Horses and me just never did get along."

Rob said, "If you were a bull rider, I guess you know Elmo, the clown?"

"Jack Babcock? Sure, everybody knows Elmo. Past his prime these days, but he was the best once. Only reason they let Elmo work the Prescott Rodeo is 'cause he lives in Prescott. Poor guy, he's on hard times these days. I don't know how he's getting by."

"He sure saved me from getting stomped yesterday," Rob said.

He broke off as the horses in the corral suddenly began snorting and rearing. And then he noticed that Alan had crawled through the rails and was moving toward the horses. He had removed his Stetson and was waving it at the animals. They were spooked.

Into Rob's mind came a chilling image of the boy falling among the rearing animals. His mind flashed to the rodeo arena yesterday as he lay helpless under the slashing hooves of the rearing horse that had just thrown him.

Now Jonas saw what was happening. "Alan! Get away!"

Unheeding, Alan kept going, waving the hat.

CHAPTER 3

Jonas shouted his son's name again and started to climb the rail fence. Rob was already over the top. He vaulted to the ground on the other side and hit the ground running. The horses were milling about in a panic now. At any second they could bolt and stampede over the child.

Rob reached the boy and scooped him up in his arms. He managed to dodge out of the way of a panicked horse at the same time. In doing so, he lost his balance and fell to his knees. He was up almost instantly and running toward the corral gate.

Jonas was running toward them. When he saw that his son was safe in Rob's arms, he changed direction. He had reached the gate and had it open by the time Rob reached it. Rob dashed through the gate, and Jonas closed it behind them.

Rob set Alan on his feet. The boy looked both bewildered and frightened at the same time.

Jonas seized him by the arm, shaking him. "What were you thinking, doing a stupid thing like that?" Jonas demanded. "How many times have I told you how easy it is to spook a horse?"

Staring down into Alan's face, Rob had an intuitive flash. He drew Jonas aside and spoke softly close to the man's ear. "I think I know what made him do it, Jonas. I'm a professional bronc rider—at least as far as the boy knows. He was showing off for me."

Jonas looked over at his son, who was standing with his head down, staring at the ground. He said, "You may be right, Rob. But even so, it was a fool thing to do."

He stepped to Alan. "Alan, look at me." The boy glanced up fearfully. "You know you just did a dumb thing. You also know that I hardly ever lay a hand on you. But if you ever do a thing like that again, I'll paddle your rear until you can't sit down for a week! You understand what I'm saying?"

The boy was close to tears. He whispered, "I'm sorry, Dad. I didn't think."

Jonas nodded. "That's plain enough. But think next time, okay? Now you run on back to the house and think about what you've done."

Without another word Alan scampered off toward the main house. Jonas stared after him for a moment. Then he said, "I've tried to teach him a healthy respect for animals. At least I thought I did. But you're right, Rob. He's just a boy, and it's natural for a boy to want to show off." He became brisk. "Let me show you the rest of the place."

The last thing Jonas showed Rob was two small house trailers behind the horse barns. "I never built a bunkhouse for the hands. I don't keep that many around. I can hire all the help I need who live around close. Right now neither of the trailers is occupied. So take your pick."

Rob said, "Suits me just fine."

"The trailers have cooking facilities. Can you cook for yourself?"

Rob laughed. "Good enough so I won't starve."

"It's too much of a chore for Marge to set meals for a bunch of cowhands. On occasion we do serve dinner for whoever is living on the ranch at the time."

Rob said, "That sounds great to me, Jonas."

They inspected the trailer Rob was to use. It was small but roomy enough for one or two people. There was a kitchen, a dining nook, one bedroom, and a bath. There was even a small television set. Everything was neat and well-tended. The only thing it didn't have was a telephone.

"This is great, Jonas. I've paid good money to stay in motel rooms much worse than this."

As they left the trailer, Jonas said, "Take the rest of the day to get settled in. First thing in the morning I'll show you the horses I want you to break and train for calf roping and bulldogging."

*   *   *

The next week, Rob worked hard. He had little trouble breaking the horses to riding, but teaching them the other tricks of the trade was harder. They had to learn to run true during the roping events with a cowboy on their backs. They also had to learn to properly carry a rider while bulldogging steers. In true horse style, some of them did not want to do this, and they showed it. In truth, Rob had to train himself as well as the horses. Fortunately, Jonas wasn't around most of time to observe how green Rob was at the job.

During the week, Rob learned a great deal more about stock contractors. They supplied bucking horses, bulls, steers, calves, and saddle horses. Jonas Greene, of course, was a stock contractor—or at least, trying to become one.

The contractor had to do more than supply the stock. He also had to evaluate his animals and pass that information on to the performers. He was supposed to be honest with the performers, but that wasn't always the case. It was important for the rodeo cowboys to know everything possible about the animals they rode or worked with.

One performer put the ideal relationship into a few words. "The relationship is much like that between a race car driver and his mechanic, Hardesty. The mechanic knows the car much better than the driver. But the mechanic isn't the one out there driving the car around the track. Same with a stock contractor. He knows his stock or should know his stock, but he isn't riding the animals."

It didn't take Rob long to conclude that Jonas Greene was struggling to survive. He had been trying in vain for years to get the stock contract with the Prescott Rodeo. He had contracts with a few smaller rodeos throughout the state, but he wasn't getting rich at it.

All of this information was very interesting, Rob concluded. But it wasn't much help in finding the people who were rustling stock in the area.

Unless Jonas was doing it himself. . . . Could he be so close to the edge of bankruptcy that he was stealing cattle and horses to survive? Rob knew that such a possibility existed. But he couldn't see Jonas Greene as a rustler.

He finally decided to keep that idea on the back burner while he continued his investigation in other areas.

Alan dogged his heels every day that week. He watched closely as Rob worked with the horses. Rob had other duties besides training the horses for roping events. He was also supposed to decide which horses were suitable for the bareback and saddle bronc riding events. Those that he judged to be good buckers he set aside. They didn't need to be broken; just the opposite was true. The less saddle-broke they were, the better they were for rodeos. Good rodeo bucking horses were born that way.

The boy pestered him with questions. In the beginning Rob was annoyed by this; it interfered with his work. But as the days passed, he relaxed and even came to enjoy it. The boy was very bright and active, as full of energy as a wind-up toy. He soaked up information like a sponge.

Every day after Rob had finished his other work, he gave Alan at least an hour of riding instructions. He let him ride only the gentlest of horses. Alan was eager to learn and obeyed Rob's teachings to the letter. But close to the end of the week, the boy began to complain. Rob had just given Alan a ride on an older horse. The animal was so old that breaking into a gallop would probably exhaust him. Alan did manage to urge the animal into a trot. When he came back to the railing where Rob was waiting, he climbed down with a scowl.

"Rob, when will you let me on a horse that can move out?" he demanded angrily. "Or one that will buck? How can I ever become a bronc rider if'n I don't ride one that bucks?"

Rob laughed. "You've heard that old expression, Alan—a step at a time? Don't hurry things."

Alan scuffed his boot toe in the dirt. "You think it's 'cause I'm too little! I'm not a kid anymore!"

"Right," Rob said dryly. "In a few days, I promise. . . ."

"You do what Rob says, Alan," said a voice on the other side of the fence.

Rob turned around to see Marge Greene standing at the railing. He had been introduced to her the day he had arrived. Mrs. Greene was a tall, strapping woman in her late thirties. She was good-looking with strong features, flaming red hair, and laughing green eyes. She had a great sense of humor, and she loved her son to distraction. Rob could well understand her devotion to the boy. He was the only child the Greenes had and likely would be the only one they ever had.

Now she said with false severity, "You may think you're not still a kid, young man, but Rob and I know differently."

"Aw, Mom!" the boy said plaintively.

"Stop whining, Alan. Run along to the house now." She gestured curtly. "Go on now."

Marge Greene turned her attention to Rob. She smiled ruefully. "I've never seen Alan take to anyone like he has you, Rob. We have only one relative, Jonas and me. Jonas's brother down in Texas. Alan worships his uncle, but he only gets to see him once in a blue moon. While you . . ."

"While I'm right here," Rob said, feeling uncomfortable.

"I'm embarrassing you, aren't I?" Marge said with a laugh. "Tomorrow's Friday, Rob, last working day of the week. Jonas suggested that we have you up for dinner. Okay with you?"

Rob said, "Sounds great."

"We usually eat early." Marge smiled. "You tend to do that on a ranch. Bed early, up early. Six-thirty all right?"

Rob nodded. "I'll be there."

*   *   *

Marge Greene was a marvelous cook. She served a beef roast, browned new potatoes, and a couple of side dishes with thick slabs of cornbread. The dessert was homemade peach pie. Everything was delicious. Rob ate so much he began to feel ashamed of himself.

During dinner Jonas carried most of the conversation. He was full of his plans to become a stock contractor that would cause rodeo people to sit up and take notice.

He said, "It's not easy. It takes time and money, a great deal of money. Why, at a rodeo stock auction a couple of years ago, a bucking mare named Baldy went for just under fourteen thousand dollars! A nine-year-old gelding went for twelve thousand. I estimate that a full string of top-quality bucking stock would cost close to a million, maybe even more. A lot of bucks, Rob."

Rob listened without much interest. Over coffee and dessert, he said casually, "I've heard rumors that rustlers have been operating in the area. You had any trouble with them, Jonas?"

Jonas leaned back from the table. "Nope, they haven't hit me. Not yet anyway."

Alan said loudly, "Rustlers wouldn't dare hit our ranch. Daddy has a big shotgun. He'd blast 'em to smithereens! I just betcha he would!"

"My, aren't we the bloodthirsty one!" Marge said. "I don't like that kind of talk, son."

"Well, he would!" Alan said.

"Let's not get carried away, Alan," Jonas said absently. "It'll likely never come to that anyway. I don't have enough cattle to interest rustlers."

"But you do have horses," Rob said. "You said yourself that they were more valuable than cattle."

Jonas nodded. "That's true. But they're harder to steal and to sell than cattle. For one thing, most of my horses are kept in pastures near the ranch. They're not miles away, spread all over, like the cattle." He took a sip of coffee. "But you're right, rustlers are operating around here. Guy up north a ways lost some fifty head just last week. Almost every week I hear about some ranch getting hit."

"Can't the sheriff's people do anything about the rustling?" Rob asked.

"Oh, they investigate, do what they can. But it's hard. The only way they can catch the rustlers, unless they get lucky, is to stake out all the ranches in the county. They don't have the manpower for that."

Rob nodded. "And they probably don't consider rustling a serious enough crime to call for too much time and effort, and the extra manpower like you say."

"That could be, I don't know. I do know that most people look at you funny when you mention rustlers. They say it sounds like something out of an old cowboy movie." Jonas gave a shrug. "It is a little hard to believe, rustlers operating in this day and age."

*   *   *

Rob was glad that he didn't have to work on the ranch on the weekends. Working with the horses was an absorbing job, but it wasn't getting him anywhere in his investigation. He had wanted a place to use as a base. Now that he had that, he needed to get around the countryside more.

On Saturday night he put on clothes to fit his role as a working cowboy out for a night on the town. He wore a fairly new Stetson, a tan shirt with pearl buttons, clean jeans, and cowboy boots.

On the main highway he drove toward Chino until he came to a tavern with a neon light blinking—Cowboy's Haven. He pulled into the parking lot. Gravel rattled like buckshot against the undercarriage of the pickup. The lot was more than half full. He got out of the pickup and went in. He noticed with a grin that almost all the vehicles on the lot were pickups.

When he opened the door, he was greeted with a blast of noise. Voices were loud, and the jukebox was cranked up to high volume. A country-western tune was playing. The place was packed and filled with smoke. Rob was met with the odors of spilled beer and other drinks and a heavy underscent of sweat. He wormed his way to an empty place at the bar and ordered a beer.

Sipping the beer, he leaned his back against the bar and looked slowly around the room. Most of the men and women he saw were dressed pretty much as he was. There was a small, cleared space in front of the jukebox that served as a dance floor. Several couples were on the floor.

Rob thought hard as his gaze moved slowly around the noisy room. How was he going to do this? He couldn't strike up a conversation with a total stranger and ask questions about stock rustling. If he only knew someone . . .

Then his glance went back to the dance floor as something belatedly struck a chord. There! All the men except one were either bareheaded or wore cowboy hats. The exception wore a baseball cap with the bill turned around to the back of his head. At the moment the man's back was turned to Rob. He was dancing with a tall, good-looking woman with blonde hair. Then he swung his partner around, and Rob saw his face. The face was faintly familiar. Then Rob recognized the man. It was the truck driver Rob had met earlier in the week, the driver of the stalled eighteen-wheeler on the road to the Greene Ranch. What was his name? Yes, Troy Simms.

Just then the music stopped. The dancers began to break up. Simms and the woman with him moved to a small table on the edge of the dance floor. They sat down, and Simms motioned to a waitress.

Rob waited until the waitress served the couple. Then he walked toward the table, carrying his half-finished beer. He started past the table. Then he stopped and turned back, as if suddenly recognizing the truck driver.

"Hey, Mr. Simms!" he said. "Did you have any more trouble with your eighteen-wheeler?"

Simms glanced up. His eyes were blurry, and he stared for a moment without recognition. Then he said in a slurred voice, "Hey, if it ain't the Good Samaritan! It's . . ." He snapped his fingers.

"Rob, Rob Hardesty," Rob said.

"Right, Rob." Simms gestured broadly. "Sit down, Rob, sit down. Let me buy you a brew."

Rob hesitated. "Well, just for a minute."

There was an empty chair at the table behind him. Rob pulled it over and sat down.

Simms was leaning across the table. He swayed a little, and Rob realized that the man had had a great deal too much to drink.

In the same slurred voice Simms said to the blonde woman, "Rig broke down early in the week. Guy here stopped to see if he could help. Ain't many guys would do that these days." Again he gestured with his big hand, almost knocking his beer bottle over. "Meet my wife, Joy. Rob, meet Joy." Simms laughed drunkenly. "Joy of my life, my wife."

Joy Simms said coolly, "Don't mind Troy, he's had more than a couple." She held out her hand. "Glad to meet you, Rob."

Rob shook her hand. "Same here." Up close the woman didn't seem quite so attractive. She was wearing far too much makeup. Her mouth was a slash of scarlet, and she had tried in vain to hide the lines in her face. Her blue eyes were hard and had an alcoholic bleariness.

"What do you mean, woman?" Simms said belligerently. "You saying I'm snookered?"

Joy Simms said, "You should be used to me saying that by now."

"Yeah, you're always flapping your mouth about something," Simms said in a growling voice. He scowled at her, his face red with anger. Then he looked around until he spotted a waitress and waved her over.

Rob held up the beer bottle. "I haven't finished this one yet."

"Then you have some catching up to do." To the waitress Simms said, "A beer for my friend, and another round for me and my old lady while you're at it."

The waitress left, and Simms looked at Rob. "You live around here, Rob?"

Rob nodded. "I just started at the Greene Ranch. I was on my way there when we met."

"Cowhand, are you?"

"No, I'm training some horses for Mr. Greene."

"Yeah, I know old Jonas." Simms laughed shortly. "Guy's been trying to get out of the cattle business and into rodeo stock contracting."

"So he told me." Rob saw his chance. "Might be a good idea, what with all the cattle rustling that's going on."

Simms blinked at him with a wary expression. "Rustling? What rustling?"

"It's getting pretty bad, the way I hear it," Rob said with an innocent look. "You must have heard about it."

"Don't know anything about cattle rustling. I drive a truck for a living."

"But you drive a cattle truck," Rob pointed out. "That means you're in the business. You must know what's going on."

Simms leaned toward him, his face reddening. His breath stank of alcohol. "You accusing me of lying, buddy?"

"I wasn't accusing you of anything."

"Sounds like it to me. . . ."

His wife interrupted, "Take it easy, Troy."

He waved a hand at her. "You keep out of this, woman." His gaze had never left Rob. His face was dark red now, his eyes bulging. "Or maybe you're accusing me of rustling?"

Rob felt a jolt of unease. It was clear that Simms was on the edge of losing it. He held up his hands. "Like I said, I'm not accusing you of anything."

"Sure as hell sounds like it."

Without warning, Simms seized Rob's nearly empty beer bottle. He smashed it on the edge of the table. The bottle broke just below the neck, making a lethal weapon. Simms lurched to his feet and jabbed the jagged edges of the bottle at Rob's face.

Startled, Rob leaned away from it. "Hey, I'm not looking for trouble!"

"Sounds like it to me," Simms snarled. "Nobody calls me a liar and a thief!"

He lunged with the bottle. Light glittered off the sharp edges. Rob jumped to his feet and managed to dodge aside.

But Simms was moving toward him again. There was little room to get out of his way on the crowded floor. Simms might be drunk, but the broken bottle made him very dangerous.

CHAPTER 4

Rob backed up another step as Simms advanced. His back was now against the table behind him. He lifted his fists to defend himself.

At that moment a man's figure loomed behind Simms. The man was holding a raised baseball bat. Rob recognized him as the man who had been working behind the bar.

"Put down the bottle, Troy," the bartender growled. "I want no trouble in my place."

Simms turned his head. "This skunk called me a liar and a thief, Don. I can't let him get away with that."

"Not in here, Troy," the bartender said. He raised the bat a few inches. "You guys want to mix it up, take it outside. If you keep on, Troy, you'll be the one to suffer."

Simms looked back at Rob with a glower as he placed the broken bottle on the table. "Okay, cowhand. Outside it is. I'll wait in the parking lot one minute. You're not out then, I'm coming back in to whip your butt, baseball bat or not."

Simms turned without another word and pushed his way through the people gathered around watching.

Rob looked down into Joy's face. "I don't want to fight your husband, Mrs. Simms. Can't you reason with him?"

Joy shrugged her shoulders. "There's no reasoning with him when he's like this. You'd better go take your licks. Or beat the hell out of him. It doesn't matter to me, one way or another."

Rob hesitated for a few moments. He wasn't an absolutely fearless man. Snakes, for example, caused him to go into a mindless panic. But physical combat wasn't one of the things he was afraid of. He had served as an MP in the Army and had been faced with any number of nasty situations. He kept his body in excellent condition, and he was well-versed in boxing and judo. He could handle himself well, and he had never lost a fight.

Yet he never took pleasure from it, as did many men he knew. The prospect of mixing with the drunken truck driver in the bar's parking lot was distasteful to him. There must be a back entrance to the bar.

However, the thought of just slinking away was repugnant to him as well. And he was curious about one thing. Why had Simms reacted so violently when the subject of cattle rustling was brought up? Was the man actually involved in the cattle stealing? Or was his reaction just that of a man with too much to drink?

Rob sighed. There was only one way to find out. He made his way to the front entrance.

He was grateful for one thing when he stepped outside. Aside from Troy Simms leaning against a car parked by the entrance, the parking lot was empty. Rob had been afraid that word of a possible fight had spread through the crowd, and the lot would be packed with spectators.

Simms saw Rob coming. He came toward him, staggering slightly, long arms swinging by his sides. He outweighed Rob by some forty pounds and stood at least three inches above Rob's six feet.

Simms smirked. "Well, cowhand, I thought you weren't going to show up. Thought you'd snuck out the back."

"None of this is necessary, Simms," Rob said reasonably. "There's no cause for us to fight. If I offended you in some way, I apologize."

"You offended me all right," Simms growled. "Called me a liar and a cow thief!"

"You misunderstood me. I called you neither. I was just making conversation."

"That's not the way I read it." Simms stopped within arm's reach.

"Then you read it wrong. I'm puzzled as to why you're so upset. Unless you are a cattle rustler . . ."

Without warning Simms aimed a fist at Rob's head. Rob had been expecting it and sidestepped it easily. Almost losing his balance, Simms staggered past. Rob stuck out a foot and tripped the man. With an outraged grunt Simms fell face down in the gravel.

Simms lay quietly for a few moments. Then he came up off the ground like a wild animal, spitting and snarling. His eyes had a mad look as he glared at Rob. "I'm going to kill you, cowhand!" he bellowed.

He charged clumsily like a lumbering bear. Rob waited until the last second, then stepped nimbly aside. He drove a fist hard into Simms's belly as he stumbled past. Simms yelled in agony and doubled over, reeling as he tried to retain his balance. Rob moved quickly up behind him. He brought the edge of his hand down across the back of Simms's neck like an axe blade.

Simms grunted and collapsed slowly. Rob stood over him for a moment, alert and tense. But this time Simms was finished. He lay unconscious.

Rob heard a gasp behind him. He whirled around. A man and a woman stood just outside the entrance to the bar.

The woman said angrily, "You should be ashamed of yourself, taking advantage of a drunken man like that."

Rob could think of no response. He shrugged instead, spreading his hands. The man took the woman by the arm and steered her around Rob to a car parked a few feet away. They got into the car, and it roared off the parking lot.

Rob stared after the disappearing car for a moment before walking over to the prone figure. Should he walk away and leave Simms there? He didn't like to do that. Then Simms groaned and moved slightly. He would be regaining consciousness shortly. Rob knew that if he was still there when the man came to, he would have to fight him again. Simms was that kind of a man.

Rob got into his pickup and headed for the Greene Ranch. The evening had been pretty much of a disaster. He had learned nothing, and he had made a bitter enemy.

*   *   *

The next morning, Sunday, the Greenes were at church when Rob got up. He was just as glad. He was in a bad mood, and he didn't want to have to explain about last night.

He drove into Chino and ate breakfast. He got a local telephone book from the waitress and leafed through it while he ate his breakfast. Somewhat to his surprise, he found what he was looking for. A Troy Simms was listed. When the waitress came with a refill for his coffee, he asked her about the address listed for Simms.

"Troy Simms?" she asked. "Sure, I know Troy. And his wife, Joy. They come in for breakfast now and again. Their place is only about a mile from here."

She gave him directions on how to get to the Simms place. A few minutes later Rob stopped in front of the address. He realized that he might be making a mistake. Yet Simms would be sober this morning. Maybe he would listen to reason. Rob still felt bad about the fight, even if it had been forced on him, and he wanted to apologize. Maybe Simms wouldn't settle for an apology, but at least he would have tried.

The Simms place was a small house, well-kept, painted a light gray. There was a small lawn in front with several trees shading the house. There was an attached garage. The door was up, but the garage was empty. In a long driveway beside the garage sat the eighteen-wheeler that Rob had seen the morning he first met Troy Simms.

He went to the door and rang the bell. He could hear the bell ring inside, but no one came to the door. He rang the bell again. Finally he heard stirring inside and the sound of a voice calling faintly, "Just a minute!"

Shortly the door opened, and Joy Simms looked out at him. She was wearing a robe, and her hair was tousled.

"Mrs. Simms? Rob Hardesty. We met at—"

She said, "Yeah, I recognize you. At the bar last night. Sorry, I'm not tracking too well yet. Didn't get in until late and I've been sleeping in."

"Sorry if I woke you. Could I speak to your husband for a moment?"

"Can't, I'm afraid. Troy isn't here."

Rob frowned. "He isn't here?"

"Nope. He stormed back into the bar shortly after you left." She grinned impishly. "Apparently you decked him pretty good. I don't think I've ever seen him so angry. He made all kinds of threats, said he was going to kill you if he ever saw you again. Then he stomped out and drove away in our car. I had to get a ride with a friend."

"He didn't come home, call you, or anything?" Rob asked.

She shook her head. "Nope. Haven't heard or seen him since."

"I'm sorry all this happened, Mrs. Simms," Rob said. "I really don't know what I said to tick him off so. When I went outside, he left me no choice. He attacked me and I had to fight back."

Joy Simms shrugged. "Don't worry about it. Troy can turn stone stupid when he's drinking. He'll come home eventually, his tail dragging."

"Well . . ." Rob hesitated. "Look, when he does come home, tell him I came by, and that I'm sorry this ever happened."

"I'll tell him." She smiled softly. "That's nice of you, Mr. Hardesty. I'll be sure to tell him. Thanks for dropping by."

She closed the door in his face. Rob got in his pickup and drove off. He was puzzled. Something about this whole episode bothered him. It didn't feel quite right.

He debated with himself about what to do with the rest of the Sunday. He had no leads to follow up; there was nothing he could think of to do that would further his investigation.

He toyed briefly with the thought of calling Stanley Morgan. Morgan had made it clear that he was available to his operatives seven days a week, twenty-four hours a day. The only papers that undercover agents carried on their persons were in their cover names. Sometimes agents got into situations where this might cause a problem.

"Any time it's important that you be identified, call me, Rob." Morgan had told him this in the beginning. "I'm always available, no matter what time."

Yet this was certainly not an emergency. And Rob didn't feel that he should call his supervisor on Sunday just for advice or just to chat.

In the end he drove back to Greene Ranch. It was the middle of the afternoon now, and the Greenes had returned from church. Rob parked the pickup by his trailer and changed into work clothes. He strolled over to the pasture next to the barn and leaned on the railing. He'd been here only a week, but some of the horses had become familiar with him. Now two of them trotted over, sticking their noses through the railing in search of treats.

Rob laughed. "Sorry, I have nothing to offer. You guys are spoiled, you know that?"

"Here, I brought something."

It was Alan. He was carrying two halves of an apple. Holding one half in each hand, he thrust them through the railing. The apple pieces were gobbled up immediately.

"Oh-ho, you're the one doing the spoiling," Rob said with a laugh.

"Daddy always says that if you're good to horses, they'll be good to you," Alan said with an earnest face.

Rob nodded. "I suppose there's more than a little truth in that."

"Rob . . ." The boy's face was turned up to him. "Are you part Indian?"

"Yes, I am, Alan. Half Navajo."

"How can you be half something?"

As Rob searched for an answer, a voice said behind him, "The proper word, son, is Native American. And it's rude, asking a question like that."

Smiling, Rob said, "Not really rude, Jonas. But maybe a little difficult to answer."

Alan said, "I'm sorry, Rob. I didn't mean nothing."

"I'm sure you didn't, Alan." Rob touched the boy on

the shoulder. "So you have nothing to be sorry for."

Alan said eagerly, "Then will you give me some riding lessons?"

"Not now, son," Jonas said. "It's Rob's day off. Can't expect him to work on Sunday."

"I don't mind," Rob said. "It's really not work . . ."

"No," Jonas said firmly. "Boy's got to learn he can't always have his way."

Alan fell quiet, sulking. They all leaned on the rail, gazing at the horses grazing in the meadow.

Rob said casually, "Jonas, do you know a man named Troy Simms?"

"Name sounds familiar. Drives a truck, doesn't he?"

"Yes. A cattle truck."

"Oh, yeah. I know Simms. Not all that well, but I know him. Why do you ask?"

Rob said, "I ran into him in a bar last night. He was smashed, and he took offense to something I said. I really don't know what riled him. But he insisted that I fight him."

"And did you?" Jonas asked.

"I had no choice. It wasn't much of a fight. He was too drunk."

Jonas nodded. "Now I remember. I recall he has a reputation as a troublemaker. Bad temper."

"That's what his wife said," Rob said. "Maybe that explains it."

They fell silent again. After a little, Jonas began to talk about his plans to become a stock contractor. Rob only half listened. As soon as good manners permitted, Rob excused himself and went to his trailer.

The small TV in the trailer brought in a picture of

rather poor quality. Rob watched a few innings of a baseball game. The game reminded him of Troy Simms and his baseball cap worn backward.

He was still puzzled as to the reason Simms had erupted into a fit of anger. Drunkenness didn't explain it to Rob's satisfaction. Was it really possible that Simms was involved in the cattle rustling? He owned the cattle truck, a perfect means of transporting stolen stock.

After the baseball game was over, he cooked his supper. He baked a potato and broiled a small steak. Rob was far from a gourmet cook, but he had learned how to cook simple but nourishing food.

By the time he was finished eating, it was dark. He turned on the TV again but couldn't find any program that interested him. He switched off the TV and settled in with a book. The book wasn't all that interesting, either, and he fell asleep.

He was awakened some time later by a noise outside the trailer. He cocked his head, listening. It sounded like the clop of a horse's hooves.

He picked up a flashlight and hurried outside. The sound was a few yards away. He hurried toward it. He swung the beam of the flashlight around the area.

It was a horse, but it certainly wasn't a horse from the pasture. There was a rider on its back. He walked toward the animal, calling out, "Hello? Who are you?"

There was no answer. Now he was close enough to see that the rider was slumped over in the saddle. Rob caught the reins and brought the horse to a stop.

Then Rob noticed that the rider was tied to the saddle. He reached up and lifted the man's head. In the light from the flashlight, he found himself looking into the face of Troy Simms. There was a bullet hole between his eyes.

CHAPTER
5

For a moment Rob felt faint. This couldn't be happening! How could Troy Simms have ended up dead, tied onto a horse, and only yards from his trailer?

He shook his head sharply. First things first.

He aimed the flashlight beam at Simms's face again, looking closely. Other than the bullet wound, there were no marks on his face. Wait! Rob paused with the beam on the dead man's cheek. There was a perfect imprint of lips on the cheek, outlined in red lipstick.

Rob let the head drop back into its original position, then examined the ropes pinning Simms to the saddle. Simms's hands were tied behind him, and a rope had been lashed around his torso, extending down under the belly of the horse. And his booted feet were tied into the saddle stirrups.

Standing back, Rob thought hard. Should he untie the body and ease it to the ground now? Or should he leave it just like it was for the police to inspect? Rob knew that he might be destroying evidence by untying him. At the very least the police would want to take pictures of Simms in his present position.

A shout from the direction of the house alerted him. He glanced that way and saw a flashlight beam bobbing toward him.

The shout came again, "Rob, is that you?"

"Yes, Jonas. Something's happened," Rob answered.

Jonas Greene came hurrying up, out of breath. "I thought I heard a horse out here. What's happened?"

In answer Rob moved the beam of his flashlight to the man on the horse.

"Dear God!" Jonas exclaimed. "Is he—?"

"Yes, Jonas, he's dead. He's been shot."

"Shot!" Jonas moved closer, examining the ropes binding Simms to the saddle. "And he's been tied to the horse?"

"It would seem so, Jonas."

"But why, for Heaven's sake?" Jonas demanded.

"That I can't answer."

The rancher asked, "Do you know who the man is?"

"Yes, it's Troy Simms."

"The truck driver you mentioned this afternoon?" Jonas was staring at him. "The one you had the fight with?"

"The same one."

Jonas said tightly, "That strikes me as a hell of a coincidence, Rob."

Rob nodded. "I can't argue with that."

"Well . . ." Jonas sighed heavily. "I reckon we'd better untie him and get him—"

Rob interrupted, "No, we'll leave him just like he is.

The police won't be happy if we don't."

"Why is that?"

"I think it's called disturbing the crime scene," Rob said wryly.

Jonas stared. "How do you know that?"

Rob gave a shrug. "Watching all those crime shows on TV, I guess."

Jonas stared at him for another moment, then sighed again. "Okay, we'd better call them. Want me to do it? Or you?"

"You do it, Jonas. I'll stay here and see that the horse doesn't wander off."

Jonas nodded, started to speak again, then changed his mind. He turned on his heel and walked toward the house.

*   *   *

Two sheriff's vehicles arrived a half hour later. Two uniformed officers were in one. The other held an investigating officer in plain clothes. He introduced himself as Bill Miller. He was a slender man in his early forties with a narrow face, thinning brown hair, and cynical gray eyes.

"I'm Rob Hardesty," Rob said.

"You work here, Mr. Hardesty?"

"Yes. Temporarily. I'm training horses for Mr. Greene; I only started this week."

Miller glanced over at Jonas Greene, who was standing nearby, then back at Rob. Rob told himself to be careful; those cynical eyes didn't miss much.

The detective said, "That what you do for a living?"

"Not really. My first time at it." Rob smiled. "But Mr. Greene was willing to take a chance on me."

"So what do you do ordinarily?"

Rob shrugged. "A little rodeoing the past few months. But I wasn't setting the world on fire, decided it was time I quit. I've done this and that, some cowboying, driving a truck. Whatever."

Miller looked at the dead man on the horse. One of the other men was taking pictures with a flash camera.

"This is going to be a weird one," Miller said absently. He looked again at Rob. "Suppose you tell me what happened here, Mr. Hardesty."

"Well, I can't tell you very much. I was in the trailer . . ." Rob indicated the house trailer with a jerk of his thumb. "I was reading, but I dozed off. The sound of a horse outside woke me. I came out, thinking maybe one of Mr. Greene's horses had gotten out, and found this."

"Did you touch anything?"

Rob said, "The only thing I did was check and make sure he was dead."

The sound of an approaching vehicle interrupted him. An ambulance was pulling in behind the police cars. Another unmarked car arrived with the ambulance. A man got out carrying a black bag.

"'Bout time," Miller muttered. "Medical examiner."

The investigator walked over to meet the man with the bag. They stood talking for a moment, then went over to the horse. Rob looked over at Jonas Greene, thinking of going over to talk. But the look Greene returned was cool, definitely unfriendly, so Rob stayed where he was.

Now the sheriff's investigator walked back to Rob. "Did you know the dead man, Mr. Hardesty?"

"Yes, sir, I did," Rob answered with extreme reluctance.

Miller's eyes narrowed. "You did?"

Rob sighed. "Yes, I met him twice. His name was Troy Simms, and he drove a cattle truck. An eighteen-wheeler."

"Would you relate the circumstances of those two meetings?"

"The first was Monday of this week. I was on my way to the ranch here. Simms's truck was stalled on the road up a ways. We introduced ourselves. I asked if I could be of assistance, and he said that a mechanic was on the way. That was the extent of that meeting."

"And the second?" Miller said in a hard voice.

"That was last night, at a bar over on the highway. The Cowboy's Haven."

Miller made a sour face. "Yeah, I know the place. A down and dirty honky-tonk. What happened there?"

Rob considered lying, but it would only be worse for him when Miller found out. And he was certain to find out.

He said, "We had a fight, I'm sorry to say."

Miller's gaze had never left Rob's face. "What did you fight about?"

"That's the odd thing." Rob gave a shrug. "I'm not sure."

"You're not sure? You had a fight with a guy and you don't know the reason? Were you drunk?"

"No, but Simms was," Rob said. "That's the only thing I can think of that might have brought it on. He was drunk and belligerent. He somehow thought that I had called him a liar."

Miller asked, "And had you?"

"Of course not! I had no reason. His wife said that Simms always got belligerent when he'd had too much to drink."

"His wife was there? She heard it all?"

"Yes, she did." Rob thought of telling the investigator about his visit to the Simms house this morning. Then he recalled the advice good defense lawyers gave their clients: Never volunteer information during an interrogation. Just answer the question and nothing more. Rob felt a cold shiver at the thought. Why was he thinking like a suspect being grilled?

Miller asked, "What's the wife's name?"

"Joy, Joy Simms."

"I'll have a talk with her about the fight."

"She didn't see the actual fight," Rob said quickly. "The bartender insisted we take the fight outside to the parking lot. She stayed inside at their table."

"How did the fight turn out?" Miller demanded.

"Simms was too drunk to fight," Rob said with a shrug. "It didn't last long." He laughed shortly. "As the saying goes, he didn't lay a glove on me."

Miller studied him keenly for a moment. "Own a gun, Mr. Hardesty?"

Rob made a startled sound. "No, I don't. Am I under suspicion here?"

Miller smiled grimly. "Let's put it this way. . . . You're here, you knew the victim, and you exchanged harsh words with the victim. But this is just the beginning of my investigation. Who knows what will turn up? I'm not going to arrest you, not now, but you will have to come down to the station and make a full, signed statement." His attitude softened slightly. "Not now. Sometime in the morning will be okay."

Rob nodded. "Of course. You're welcome to search my trailer for the murder weapon if you're so inclined."

"I doubt very much if you'd hide the murder weapon in your living quarters," Miller said. "But I will have a man search as a matter of routine."

Miller turned away, striding over to the horse. They had removed the body from the animal now and had Simms stretched out on a blanket on the ground. The man from the medical examiner's office was on one knee beside the body. Miller stood over him, talking quietly.

Rob walked over to where Jonas stood watching the proceedings. "I'm sorry that this had to happen, Jonas."

Jonas turned to him. "Not your fault, I suppose. But one thing I can't understand. Whoever killed Simms, for whatever reason, why in heaven's name did he tie him on a horse?"

"I have no idea, Jonas," Rob said slowly. But he had been thinking about it, and he could see only one answer. Simms's killer must be sending him a warning. Yet how could anyone possibly know that he was investigating the stock thefts? Could it mean that he was getting close to the rustling ring?

Rob sighed to himself. If he was indeed getting close to discovering the rustlers, he certainly didn't know about it! But what other reason could trigger such an action?

*   *   *

Rob was back from the sheriff's office in Prescott by noon the next day. He had made his statement and left without once seeing Bill Miller, the sheriff's investigator. Rob had made his statement to another deputy. He had thought of asking about Miller, but that would only stir the waters. As far as he was concerned, Rob would be just as happy if he never saw Bill Miller again.

Back at the ranch, he changed into his work clothes and went to the pasture. He rounded up the horses he was training and began working them. He worked hard for the rest of the afternoon and was pleased by the progress he was making. He decided that he was good enough to make a living at training rodeo stock if it became necessary.

He grinned to himself. It might well become necessary to find other employment if he didn't make some progress with the case soon. The one person who possibly knew something about the rustling had wound up murdered, and Rob hadn't a clue as to which way to turn next.

He hadn't seen any of the Greenes all day. Jonas's pickup

was gone, so the rancher must be off on business. But his wife was home, and since school was out for the summer, Alan was likely home as well. Ordinarily the boy would be out here watching Rob work and pestering him to death.

The day grew to a close, and Alan didn't show up. Jonas drove up in his pickup shortly after four and parked in front of the ranch house. He got out and went into the house without so much as a glance toward the corrals. Alan wasn't with him.

Neither Jonas nor his son had come out of the house by the time Rob quit work for the day. Clearly, they were avoiding him like he had the plague.

In the trailer he took a shower and put on fresh clothing. He debated with himself for a few moments. He wondered if he should call his supervisor and report on what had happened so far. Since the trailer didn't have a telephone, Jonas had told Rob that he could always use the phone at the main house when he needed to make a call. But Rob needed privacy when he called Morgan.

He could go out for supper and call from a pay phone. The supervisor expected a report when some progress was made or when something unusual happened. Rob figured that murder certainly qualified as something unusual.

But he was tired. He'd had almost no sleep last night after the police left the ranch. He finally decided that the call could be postponed until tomorrow.

He rummaged in the small refrigerator for the makings of a meal. He found some hamburger meat, frozen french fries, and the makings of a salad. He made a mental note to go food shopping tomorrow; that would give him an excuse to go into town.

After eating the skimpy meal, he sat down before the TV set. It was rerun season, and there wasn't even a ballgame on. After watching a dull program for almost an hour, Rob dropped off to sleep, just like he had last night.

This time it was a loud knock on the trailer door that awakened him. He awoke with a start, and it took a minute for him to even realize where he was.

The knock sounded again, louder this time. Rob got to his feet and opened the door. Bill Miller, the sheriff's investigator, stood on the stoop. Behind him Rob saw an unmarked car parked behind his pickup. Behind it was another vehicle with two men in it.

They must have driven up very quietly, Rob thought. He felt a small jolt of alarm.

"Mr. Hardesty," Miller said, "I have a few questions. May I come in?"

Rob stepped back. "Of course."

Miller came in warily, looking around. Rob motioned to the small couch, and the investigator sat down. Rob sat across from him.

Miller said, "I've spent the day interviewing witnesses to the brawl you had at the bar." He took out a notebook and flipped it open. "I talked to one couple, a Mr. and Mrs. Price, who came out just as the fracas took place. They overheard a threat Simms made to you." Miller glanced up. "Simms said that he would kill you."

Rob shrugged. "That was the liquor talking."

Miller's look was skeptical. "Why didn't you relate this to me last night?"

"I didn't think it was important. Just a drunk spouting off."

"I see. I also interviewed Mrs. Simms." Miller looked down at his notebook. "She told me that Simms came into the bar after he recovered consciousness. She said he told her that he intended to kill you." Miller glanced up. "She also told me that you came by her house yesterday looking for her husband. Why did you do that?"

Rob was beginning to have a bad feeling about this. "I

thought that maybe if I apologized to him, he might—"

Miller cut him off. "Apologize? Last night, you said you had nothing to apologize for."

"I didn't, not really," Rob said. "But I thought that if I talked to him sober, it might clear the air, that he would realize he had misunderstood me."

"Why didn't you tell me that you'd driven out to his house?"

"I didn't think it had anything to do with his death."

Miller stood up. "Any little thing can be important to a murder investigation." His voice hardened. "You know what I think, Mr. Hardesty? I think that you went looking for him, that you found him after you talked to his wife, that you then killed him before he could kill you."

Rob said angrily, "That's ridiculous!"

Miller said formally, "I have to ask you to come down to the station with me, Mr. Hardesty."

Rob shot to his feet. "You're arresting me? You have no grounds for that!"

"I have enough to hold you. You're a transient, apt to flee at any time. You had opportunity, and now I've discovered that you had a motive. The means, the gun you used to kill him, we're still looking for, but I'm sure we'll find it."

"Motive? Your motive won't hold up. As for opportunity, I was here in my trailer all evening!"

"So you say, Mr. Hardesty. I have only your word for that. You were alone, so there's no one to back you up. I'll read you your Miranda rights now." Miller took a card from his pocket and began to read in a monotone. "You have the right to remain silent. Anything you say can and will be used against you . . ."

CHAPTER 6

The room was small, and the walls were painted a depressing green. Rob had been looking at those walls for over two hours. He had been questioned by both Bill Miller and another man. Rob had previously been relieved of all personal items and fingerprinted.

He knew that his fingerprints were on file. It would be only a matter of time before he was identified as Rob Harding. Miller had informed him that he had the right to have an attorney present, but Rob had refused. He knew no attorneys, and he certainly didn't want a court-appointed one. Besides, he was sure they didn't have enough evidence to hold him for long. He could stand up to their interrogation until the morning. Then he would call Stanley Morgan. Perhaps they would only hold him for an hour or so, and then there would be no need to contact Morgan at all.

In that he was wrong. At the end of the second hour of interrogation, Miller leaned back tiredly. He sighed and scrubbed a knuckle across his eyes.

He smiled faintly. "I have to say one thing, Hardesty, you're a hard nut to crack."

The investigator's use of Rob's cover name told him that his prints still hadn't been identified. He said, "Did you ever consider that I might be innocent?"

Miller said, "I always view a suspect as innocent until I have enough hard evidence to prove otherwise. But that doesn't mean you're not still a suspect." He got to his feet. "Let's call it a night, what do you say?"

Rob also got up. "That mean I'm free to go?"

"Nope," Miller said with a shake of his head. "Not yet. Ever spend a night in a jail cell?"

"No, I never have."

"In my opinion every man should experience it once in his life. Might keep you out of trouble later."

The experience wasn't as bad as Rob had expected. He was the only occupant of the cell. The bunk had a thin mattress, and he was provided with a pair of blankets. He was convinced that he wouldn't sleep, but he went to sleep at once. He slept soundly until he was awakened at seven by a jailer with a breakfast tray.

Even the breakfast wasn't half bad.

He had just finished the meal when a man came to take him back to the interrogation room. Bill Miller was waiting inside.

Rob groaned. "More questions? When will you give up?"

"I can hold you legally for seventy-two hours. And yes, I have some more questions."

Rob didn't sit down. "I suppose you've had men searching

the grounds around the trailer for the murder weapon?"

"Yes, I have."

Rob grunted. "And you didn't find it, did you?"

"No, but that doesn't mean anything. You could have tossed it anywhere."

"How many times do I have to tell you that I don't have a gun. . . ." Rob broke off with a sigh. "I'm allowed one phone call. This farce has gone on long enough. I want to make the call. Now!"

"You could have made your call last night." Miller got out of the chair. "Come along."

He led Rob down the corridor to a bank of pay phones against one wall. Miller backed off to lean against the wall a few feet away. Rob got the operator and made a collect call to the task force office in Phoenix. He was put through to Stanley Morgan immediately.

"Rob! I've been wondering why you haven't called," Morgan said. "I'm curious. Why the collect call?"

Rob said, "I'm in jail, Mr. Morgan."

"In jail! What's the deal?"

Quickly, Rob filled his supervisor in on what had happened.

Morgan was silent for a moment in thought. "You haven't told the sheriff's investigator who you are?"

"I thought it would be better coming from you. I would have called earlier, but I thought they'd let me go before this."

"Okay. Give this man, Bill Miller, my number and have him call me from his own phone," Morgan said. "You'll be out within the hour, I promise. Then call me back and fill me in in more detail."

Rob hung up the phone. There was a pad and pencil

on the wall beside the phone. He jotted down the supervisor's number, tore off the slip of paper, and held it out to Miller. "Call this number."

Miller took the paper and stared at it dubiously. "What's this?"

"Just call it, please. The man you'll be talking to is Stanley Morgan. He heads a state government agency. He'll straighten this mess out."

Miller's stare was penetrating. "This better not be some game you're running on me, Hardesty."

"No game. Just make the call."

The investigator shrugged in resignation. "Okay, but if this is a waste of my time, I'll come down on you hard."

Miller locked Rob in the interrogation room and left him there for almost half an hour. When he finally came to unlock the door, he looked cross as a bear.

"Why didn't you tell me you were an investigator with the task force?' he demanded.

Rob said, "Would you have believed me?"

"Probably not." Miller sighed. "Okay, Hardesty. Or Harding. Or whatever your name is. You can go. But be sure and keep in touch. Just because you work for this government guy, Morgan, doesn't mean you're all that innocent. You still could have killed Troy Simms." He smiled slightly. "Joy Simms is a cute dish and a real tease. Could be the old story. A falling out between two guys over a woman."

Rob shook his head. "Come on, Miller. You don't really believe that."

Miller gestured. "Go on. Collect your things and get the hell out of here."

At the front desk Rob collected his belongings and

signed that everything was intact. Then he left the station. At least Miller had been thoughtful enough to have one of his men drive the pickup into Prescott. Rob stopped at the first convenience store he saw and called Phoenix. He was put through to his supervisor at once.

"Thanks for getting me loose, Mr. Morgan."

"I could do no less, Rob," Morgan said. "Besides, I don't think the deputy was all that convinced of your guilt. I think he was only going through the motions."

"There's really no evidence. Just the fact that Simms was found dead in front of my trailer, and that I knew Simms and had fought with him."

Morgan asked, "Do you think this truck driver's death has anything to do with our rustlers?"

"I don't really know how," Rob said slowly. "Yet there is the fact that his body was tied to a horse and left at my trailer. He could have been killed and the body left there as a warning to me."

"Do you think someone knows you're investigating rustling activities for the task force?" Morgan asked.

"I don't know how anyone could know," Rob answered.

"Well, you'd better be very careful, just in case someone has found out in some way," Morgan said. "Call in every few days, Rob."

"I will, sir," Rob said, and hung up the phone.

It was almost noon now, and he was hungry. The jail breakfast hadn't been bad, but it had been on the skimpy side. On the way back to Chino Valley he stopped in a diner for lunch.

He lingered over two cups of coffee after finishing the meal. For some reason he was reluctant to return to the ranch. *Why was that?* he wondered. He could only come up with one answer: Greene's reaction to the events of last night. Rob had thought that he and the older man had developed a kind of friendship. Yet, Greene's attitude toward Rob had changed dramatically with Simms's death. And all without proof. So much for trust and friendship. Rob had to admit that he was more than a little hurt. He had to remind himself that this was a job, not a popularity contest.

He drained his coffee cup, then left the cafe for his pickup. He started the engine and headed for Chino Valley. He had passed the Cowboy's Haven and was a half mile down the road before something registered. The parking lot of the tavern had been nearly empty. There had been only two cars and a semi-truck cab parked there. Rob found a place to turn around and drove back to the tavern. He parked near the semi. The cab was without the trailer. Rob was sure that the truck cab was the one driven by Simms.

Rob got out of the pickup and pushed open the door of the saloon. The interior was dim. He stood for a moment just inside, waiting for his eyes to adjust to the change from the bright sunlight outside.

Two men perched on stools at the bar, beer bottles before them. Both men and the bartender were staring at Rob. In the back of the room sat a woman. She was hunched over a small table, nursing a drink. The woman was Joy Simms.

Rob walked toward her and stopped at the table. He cleared his throat. She didn't look up.

Rob said, "Mrs. Simms?"

Joy started and looked up. Her face was pale with a haunted look. Her eyes were swollen and red. She blinked at him dazedly. Then color surged into her face. "You! I heard you were under arrest."

"I was, but they released me." Rob sat down across from her. "I'm sorry about your husband, Mrs. Simms."

"I'm sure you are!" She spat the words at him. "That's why you murdered him!"

"I didn't kill him," Rob said steadily. "The police know that. That's why they let me go."

She continued as if he hadn't spoken. "I no longer loved Troy. I'm not even sure I liked him any more. But he was my husband. We'd been married for over ten years." Her eyes leaked weak tears. "I didn't want to see him dead!"

Even in her grief Joy Simms wore her heavy makeup. Her mouth was like a scarlet slash across her face. Rob thought of the imprint of lips outlined in bright red lipstick on the cheek of Troy Simms.

But what would be so unusual about Joy leaving the imprint of her lipstick on his face? She was his wife, wasn't she?

Rob asked, "Can you think of anyone who would want to kill your husband? Any enemies?"

Her eyes focused on him. They were hard, without tears now. "Why should you care? You hardly knew him, so don't be a hypocrite!"

Rob was taken aback. "That's true, I didn't. But I didn't want to see him dead, either, Mrs. Simms."

"You don't care. Nobody cares!" she said bitterly. "So why don't you drop the false sympathy and get out of here."

He stared at her, uncertain.

"Go on, get out of here!" She spat the words at him like bullets. "Leave me alone, so I can drink to his memory. Nobody else will."

Rob sat for a moment, wishing there was something he could do to ease this woman's pain. She had turned away, beckoning to the bartender for a fresh drink.

Now she looked at him with blazing eyes. "You still here?"

Rob got to his feet. "All right, I'm going. But again, I'm sorry this happened."

She snorted. "Yeah, right!"

Rob walked away. At the door he stopped to look back at Joy Simms. Her fresh drink had been served, and she threw it back with a toss of her head. If she kept drinking like that, she would be an accident waiting to happen.

Rob sighed. There was nothing he could do about it. She had made that clear enough. He got into the pickup and headed for the Greene Ranch.

Jonas's pickup was parked before the main house, but Rob saw no one outside. He toyed briefly with the thought of stopping to talk with Jonas about what had happened, but he decided to wait. There was the stink of jail about him. He drove on to the trailer.

Inside, he shed the clothes he was wearing on his way to the shower. He stayed in the shower for a long time. When he finally emerged, he felt clean again. He put on clean clothes and was just pulling on his boots when a knock sounded on the door. He went tense, a dread like ice along his spine. Was Bill Miller back to arrest him again?

He stepped to open the door. Jonas stood on the stoop. He looked uncomfortable, ill at ease.

Rob said, "Hi, Jonas. I was on my way up to see you."

"Hardesty . . ." Jonas cleared his throat. "We have to talk."

"Sure, Jonas." Rob stepped back. "Come in."

Jonas looked away. "I'd rather talk out here."

Jonas stepped off the stoop and walked a few steps away. The rancher dug into the dirt with the toe of his boot, staring off.

"What is it, Jonas?"

Jonas blurted, "I'm going to have to let you go, Hardesty. I'm sorry."

"Let me go?" Rob said. "Why? Because of the dead man and my being taken in by the police? That's all over. They had no evidence. As you can see, Jonas, they let me go."

Jonas was shaking his head. "I'm happy for you, but I'm still firing you. It's because of Alan. I can't have him around a man who's involved in a murder."

Rob looked at him unbelievingly. Could the man be serious? "But I'm not involved, Jonas!" Rob said slowly. "I just happened to find him. You might as well say that you are involved. After all, he was found on your property."

"I'm sorry." Jonas took a slip of paper from his pocket and held it out. "Here's your wages for last week. I'm adding an extra week."

Numbly, Rob took the check. "You won't change your mind?"

Jonas shook his head. "No, Hardesty. I have to ask you to be off my property by tonight. I don't want the boy seeing you again."

Jonas turned and walked away. Rob stood, check in his hand, staring after Jonas until the rancher walked out of sight around the horse barn. Nothing he had learned of Jonas Greene up to this time had led him to believe the man could be so unreasonable. What was going on here?

CHAPTER 7

It only took Rob a short time to pack his few possessions. He then drove into Prescott, where he found a motel room for the night.

He was low in spirits. He had uncovered a possible lead to the rustling operations in Troy Simms and had lost it. But even more, he felt hurt and a bit angry with Jonas Greene. The rancher had judged him guilty without a fair hearing. Rob was especially despondent over Alan. He hadn't realized how fond he had become of the boy.

The motel had a swimming pool. Rob put on a pair of swim trunks and went out to the pool. The motel was mostly empty, and he had the pool to himself. The shock of the water as he drove in jump-started his brain again. As he swam several laps in the pool, he thought about what his next move should be. Nothing brilliant came to him.

But at least he felt physically better. On his way back to his room he had to pass the office. Copies of the *Prescott Courier* were being delivered. Rob got a copy of the paper and carried it to his room. He got the ice bucket and went out to the drinks machine for a soda and a bucket of ice.

After a quick shower, he got dressed and sat down to read the paper. He didn't know what, if anything, he was looking for. It was something to do.

In the local and state section of the paper he came across an announcement: "Claude Watkins, a rancher in Paulden, is hosting a rodeo this week. All proceeds from the rodeo will go toward providing medical care for Roy Dalton. Dalton was a professional bull rider. He was seriously injured during the Prescott Rodeo. All donations will be gratefully accepted."

Rob jotted down the address. He knew that ranchers occasionally gave small rodeos with local rodeo people performing. These rodeos were mostly given for the performers to keep in practice. It was rare when prize money was given. That would probably be the case in this instance since it was a benefit rodeo.

Rob decided to attend. It would be something to pass the time, and he might make a valuable contact.

*   *   *

The headquarters for the Watkins Ranch was located north of the small town of Paulden. It was only a few hundred yards off the highway. The rodeo was about to begin when Rob drove his pickup into the parking lot. Attendance was evidently going to be heavy. There were around a hundred vehicles parked in the lot, and cars were still pulling in.

What Rob assumed was the ranch horse corral was used for an arena. Several food vendors worked the crowd. There was even a grandstand of sorts, a rickety framework with five tiers of wooden seats. The seats were already filled. The corral fence was lined with people watching through the pole railings. There were two chutes and a small viewing stand close by the chutes. A man sat alone on the viewing stand with a bullhorn. Rob later learned that this was Claude Watkins.

Rob found a spot along the railing from where he could watch the proceedings. He saw that there was a horse in one of the chutes, and a rider was climbing into the saddle.

The bullhorn boomed, "Now coming out of chute number one is Chad Burns, riding Ruby Red."

The chute gate swung open, and the red horse burst out into the arena. The animal had hardly cleared the chute when he bucked skyward. His head was down and his hooves almost met. The rider on his back whooped and raked the horse's flanks with the dull spurs. The animal bucked its way across the small arena.

Chad Burns lasted the full eight seconds and gave a good ride. Far better than anything I can do, Rob thought wryly, or likely ever will be able to do.

There were no pickup men today, Rob noted. The rider had to stay in the saddle until Ruby Red calmed down and could be kneed over to the arena gate. The gate opened, and the rider nudged the horse outside.

Again the bullhorn announced, "Good ride, Chad. I figure you for a 74 at least."

Rob had turned his head aside to watch the horse leave the arena. A voice spoke to him from on the other side of the rails: "Hardesty, isn't it? Rob Hardesty?"

Rob's head snapped around. A rodeo clown had his face stuck between two of the rails. Rob hadn't noticed a clown in the arena. Then he recognized the man behind the garish face paint. It was Elmo, Jack Babcock.

"Yes, Mr. Babcock. Rob Hardesty it is."

Elmo shook his head. "Elmo, son. Or just plain Jack. No friend of mine calls me Mister. Hurts my feelings." The painted mouth stretched wide in a grin. "Wouldn't want to hurt my feelings now, would you?"

"Never that, Elmo," Rob said with a laugh. It was hard to dislike this man who was so charming and friendly.

"That's better, Rob," Babcock said. "You're the bronc rider got thrown at the Prescott Rodeo last week, right?"

"That's me," Rob said with a nod. "You saved my life, Elmo."

Babcock shook his head. "I wouldn't go that far. At least I hope not. If I had, I'd be responsible for the rest of my life. Or so the old Chinese saying goes. I have enough responsibilities as it is." He glanced behind him. "You got a horse for today, Rob?"

"No, I haven't entered," Rob said. "I didn't even know about this rodeo until I read the notice in yesterday's *Courier.*"

"That doesn't matter. Claude's not all that formal. Giving a rodeo once in awhile for come one, come all, is a sort of a hobby for old Claude. Of course, this one is a little different. It's a benefit being given for poor Roy. Sad thing, that. He was pretty banged up." Babcock shook his head sadly and looked toward the chutes. "I see Ken Martin's about to show us a little bull riding. Better get to work. Nice to see you again, Rob. Why don't you amble over and tell Claude you want to ride a bronc?"

With flip of his hand Babcock slouched off toward the chutes. A splatter of applause came from the onlookers. He removed his tiny hat and bowed so low that he seemed to fall. Then he turned the fall into a somersault.

The crowd laughed, as did Rob.

A voice spoke behind him, "Funny guy, huh, old Elmo?"

Rob turned slowly. A man in his late thirties stood behind him. He wore the usual cowpuncher garb with an almost new white Stetson tilted back on his head. He was dark, slender, with slanted black eyes that had about as much expression as marbles. Rob thought he looked faintly familiar.

He said, "Yes, he is."

"Too bad he's over the hill." The man's gaze rested on the clown. "He was gored by a bull a couple of years ago. He hasn't been the same since. He can't work the big rodeos anymore."

"That is too bad," Rob said.

"Yeah. Name's Bertram Woods. Friends call me Buck." He grinned. "That's 'cause I never could cut it as a bronc rider. Always getting bucked off."

"I know what you mean," Rob said with a laugh. "That's the reason I've about given up rodeoing."

"You're Rob Hardesty, right?" Buck said and stuck out his hand.

"That's me." Rob shook the extended hand. He remembered now where he'd seen the other man. He had been one of the performers at the Prescott Rodeo last week, a bronc rider. He was even a worse rider than Rob. Rob recalled seeing him ride three horses; he never stayed on any of them for the required eight seconds.

"Yeah, I know," Buck said. "I saw you ride last week. I should hang up my spurs too. But every year when the Prescott Rodeo comes around, I can't resist giving it one more shot." He glanced around, lowering his voice. "Can we talk somewhere a little more private?"

"Sure," Rob said. He wondered what this was all about. Why had this Buck Woods sought him out?

Buck nodded toward an empty picnic table a few yards

away from the crowd. "How about over there?"

"Fine with me."

"I'm hungry. Didn't eat much breakfast. Buy you a hot dog and bottle of pop for your time," Buck offered.

"That isn't necessary . . ."

Buck said, "I insist."

He took Rob by the elbow and led him over to a hot dog vendor. They got two hot dogs and two cold drinks, then crossed over to the picnic table. As they ate, Buck studied Rob with those expressionless eyes.

"Heard you got arrested for killing Troy Simms," Buck finally said.

Rob blinked. "You heard about that?"

"Sure. Most everybody did, I reckon." Buck grinned slightly. "News travels fast around here. Small towns and all that."

"Well, you all heard wrong. I wasn't arrested, just held for questioning. I don't know why they even did that. The only connection I had was that Simms's body was found near my trailer," Rob said. He was angry at himself for the defensive note in his voice.

Buck's voice turned cynical. "Sure, you didn't." He leaned across the table. "Thing is, once a man's arrested, it's hard to convince people he didn't do the thing he was busted for. Like Jonas Greene."

"I told you, I wasn't arrested. I was just taken in for questioning," Rob said automatically. "And what do you mean about Jonas?"

Buck shrugged. "Well, he fired you, didn't he? That must mean he thinks you had something to do with it."

"You know about that too?" Rob said in astonishment.

"Like I said, word gets around." Buck spread his hands.

"Figured old Jonas would fire you. He's a real straight arrow. Guess you're looking for a job now?"

"Well, yes," Rob said cautiously.

"How particular are you, Rob?"

Rob frowned. "Exactly what do you mean by that?"

"How strong are your scruples?"

Rob now got a sense of where this was going. "Probably no stronger than anyone else's. I suppose it all depends."

"Man's been arrested for murder shouldn't be too particular," Buck said softly. His gaze was keen. "My hunch is this isn't the first time you've had a brush with the law. Right, Rob?"

Rob shrugged. "Right. A time or two, nothing really serious."

"What I have in mind is nothing really serious, either. Stealing a few cows and horses here and there."

"Rustling is a crime, Buck. I'd call that serious."

Buck snorted. "Rustling! You make it sound like we're in an old Western movie! And it's not serious because we've got it down to a science. There's almost no danger of getting caught. After what happened to Troy, we're short a man."

Buck peered at Rob to check for a reaction at the mention of Troy Simms. Rob managed to keep his face impassive. He said doubtfully, "I don't know . . ."

"It pays well, Rob," Buck said seductively. "Damned well. I should think that would appeal to a man who's going to have trouble finding a job, a man suspected of murder."

Rob kept a straight face, hiding his jubilation. Here was the opportunity he'd been hoping for! He remained silent for several moments, as though giving the matter deep thought.

Finally he nodded. "Okay, I'm in."

"Great!" Buck clapped him familiarly on the shoulder. "Welcome aboard, Rob. You won't be sorry. Meet me tonight at ten o'clock at this address."

He took out a pen and a scrap of paper. He scribbled on the paper and handed it to Rob. "I reckon I don't have to warn you to keep all this under your hat?"

"I may be a mite unlucky, but I'm not stupid," Rob said.

"Fine." Buck got to his feet. "I'll see you tonight then."

Rob watched the man walk away. Getting arrested for murder had its advantages after all. He grinned at the thought. He saw Buck Woods get into a pickup and drive away.

Stretching, Rob got up. He was ready to leave as well. Yet there was one thing he hadn't done. Over by the corral a table had been set up, a man sitting at it. Rob had noticed people stopping at the table and handing money or checks to the man. Evidently they were giving donations for the injured bull rider.

Rob made his way over to the table. Just before he reached it, Elmo the Clown stopped at the table. He took a roll of bills from his pocket. Rob watched in surprise as Babcock peeled ten hundred-dollar bills off the roll and gave it to the man at the table.

The man's eyebrows arched in pleased surprise. "Hey, thank you, Jack! That will be much appreciated."

"Always glad to help," Babcock said, turning away from the table. He didn't seem to notice Rob standing behind him.

Rob stepped up to the table to make his donation.

*   *   *

A half hour later, as he drove away, Rob was elated. This was the break he had been looking for, and it had dropped right into his lap!

He watched the rearview mirror carefully for a few miles to be sure he wasn't being tailed. He couldn't think of any reason he should be, yet it was wise to be careful. After all, it was more than possible that Buck Woods had followed him out here to recruit him.

Finally he pulled the pickup in before a convenience store and parked near a line of pay phones. He had discussed getting a cellular phone with his supervisor, but Morgan had been against it. Cellular phones, he had maintained, were too easily tapped into. Anytime Rob needed to call the task force office, it would be safer to use a pay phone.

At the phone Rob punched out the task force number in Phoenix. In a few moments he was talking to Stanley Morgan.

"Hello, Rob!" said Morgan's hearty voice over the phone. "Didn't expect to hear from you so soon. Not more trouble with the local authorities?"

"No, Mr. Morgan," Rob said. "But something happened a bit ago that I thought you should know about." He went on to tell his supervisor about the conversation with Buck Woods. He explained what it might mean to his investigation.

Morgan was silent for a moment after Rob was finished. "Don't you think it's a little strange that this man, virtually a stranger, should approach you and offer you a job with the rustlers?"

"Yes, it did. At first," Rob replied. "But I've been thinking about it. I think two things are involved here. First, they probably think that since I'm a suspect in a murder investigation, I would have no love for the law. They may even believe I'm guilty."

Morgan said sharply, "Why would they think that?"

"I don't know that they do. But it's been my experience that people who break the law have a tendency to believe that everyone else has the same lack of moral sense that they do."

Morgan gave a skeptical grunt. "That may be, but it has a smell to it."

"And second," Rob continued, "they're evidently short a man since Simms was killed."

"This is all awfully convenient, Rob. It makes me uneasy," Morgan said.

"But this is what we hoped would happen, Mr. Morgan," Rob said. "I was supposed to hang around up here, pretend to be a rodeo performer who isn't quite good enough to make it. Although I didn't have to pretend too hard," Rob laughed. "Anyway, I was supposed to be desperately in need of money. I had to look to be willing to work at something shady and hope I'd be approached by the rustlers. Well, it's happened. Now I've got the opportunity to get inside their operation."

Morgan said, "That's only one approach we considered, Rob. There were others less risky to you."

"I don't consider it all that risky, sir," Rob said. "No more risky than any other undercover assignment."

"Perhaps not. But be extra careful, Rob," Morgan warned. "Don't forget that a man's been murdered."

"We don't know that Simms's murder has anything to do with the stock thieves."

"No, but it would be mighty coincidental otherwise. Just be careful, Rob," Morgan said. "You've become one of my best operatives, and I don't want to lose you."

Rob laughed. "You don't have to worry about that, sir. I don't want to lose me, either."

*   *   *

It was a few minutes before ten o'clock that evening. Rob pulled the pickup into a lot before what had once been a service station. The station, located several miles north of Paulden, had clearly been abandoned for years. The building had been stripped of anything usable, and all the windows had been broken out. As Rob turned off the ignition, he could hear the scurry of rats inside. Evidently they had been alarmed by the sound of the pickup.

He only had to wait a few minutes before another pickup drove into the lot. It was this year's model and much more expensive than Rob's. It drove in the wrong way, stopping with the driver's door only a foot away from Rob.

Buck Woods grinned out the window. "Prompt, I see. I like that in a man. I'll be driving a few miles farther north on 89A, then turning left onto a side road. Our destination is about two miles in. You follow me in your rig, Hardesty. I'll keep an eye out, see that you don't get lost."

Before Rob could do more than nod, Buck slammed his pickup into gear and took off with a roar. Rob quickly started his vehicle and fell in behind him. As promised, Buck Woods turned off a few miles up the highway.

The road they turned onto was little more than two ruts left by tire tracks in the ground. It was a gravel road. It would be almost impossible for investigators to pick up tire imprints. Rob thought that whoever was behind the rustling was a very smart man.

Even so, the road was full of chuckholes, and they couldn't drive very fast. Even driving slowly, the other pickup sent up a cloud of dust. Rob had all his windows closed, yet dust seeped into the cab. He dropped back a few hundred yards to escape most of the dust. There was no danger of losing Buck's pickup, not with the haze it left in the air.

Rob was relieved when the other pickup stopped a few miles in from the main highway. When he pulled in behind it, Rob could see a big semi-truck parked in front of the other pickup. It was a cattle truck. When Rob got a good look at it, he was almost certain that it was the eighteen-wheeler that had belonged to Troy Simms. If it was Simms's truck, there no longer seemed any doubt that Simms had been involved with the rustlers.

Rob wondered if he was being hired to drive the truck. He couldn't recall having told Buck that he had driven semis for a time in the past.

He parked and got out. Buck was already out and walking toward the parked eighteen-wheeler. Before Buck reached it, the cab door opened, and someone climbed down.

Buck had left his pickup lights on. As the figure from the truck cab stepped into the spill of light, Rob was surprised to see that it was Joy Simms.

Buck immediately engaged her in conversation. Rob stepped into the light and moved toward the pair. At the sound of his footsteps, Joy Simms looked around, squinting in the bright lights. She was wearing work clothes, jeans, dark shirt, and boots, but her face was as garishly painted as always.

Astonishment and outrage registered on her face. Then she yelled, "You! What are you doing here?"

She jerked a small gun from her pocket and ran at him. She stopped a few feet away. She gripped the gun in both hands, aimed at Rob's heart. His heart was thudding in his chest like a drum—he was about to die!

"I swore to myself that if I ever ran across you again, I'd kill you for murdering Troy!" Joy raged.

CHAPTER 8

Rob was taken by surprise. He could only stand staring down into the gun barrel. It seemed to grow larger with every passing second.

Then Buck stepped up behind her, wrapping his arms around her, forcing the gun down. She cursed, flailing with her arms and legs.

Buck was laughing. "Whoa! What gives with you, woman? Why this sudden bent toward homicide?"

She spat the words out, "He killed Troy!"

"The cops don't seem to think so," Buck said. "And why should you care, anyway? You and Troy weren't what you might call lovebirds, Joy. How many times have you told me you were thinking of leaving him?"

"That doesn't matter. He was my husband," she said with heaving breath.

Rob stepped to them. He took the pistol from Joy's

grasp. He could smell alcohol on her hot breath.

"Well, don't take it out on Rob, okay?" Buck said. "He's one of us now. If I let you go, will you go back to the truck cab and behave yourself?"

Joy nodded, and Buck dropped his arms from around her. Joy gave Rob a bitter look, and for a moment he thought she was going to fly at him. Then her shoulders slumped, and she trudged back to the truck cab. She climbed the steps and slammed the heavy door loudly.

Rob gave Buck the gun. "She drives that eighteen-wheeler?"

"Sure. Handles it like a pro." Buck laughed. "She's driven it many times before on a job. Old Troy had a habit of getting too plastered to drive."

"Speaking of plastered, did you know she's been drinking?"

"Yeah, I know," Buck said with a shrug. "But there's a big difference between Joy and her late husband. She can always handle it, and she knows enough to keep her mouth shut." Buck's hard gaze met Rob's. "Troy had another bad habit. When he was drunk, he talked too much."

Rob had to wonder if Buck was aiming a not-too-subtle threat at him. He said, "I know when to keep my mouth zipped, Buck."

"Good! Words I like to hear." He clapped Rob on the shoulder. He said briskly, "Now! We're going on down this road about another two miles. I'll take the lead, Joy right behind me, and you'll follow her."

Rob nodded his agreement and went back to his pickup. Buck started his and pulled around the truck. The semi started to move, and Rob fell in behind it.

Their progress was slow. The semi had to creep along in a low gear. Even at low speed it groaned and bounced over the many potholes in the road.

It took over a half hour before they reached their destination. Rob saw the truck's rear lights suddenly flare red and come to a stop. Rob braked the pickup, then shut off the motor. The truck motor also went silent. In the sudden quiet, Rob could hear the bawling of cattle.

He got out of the pickup and walked up toward the sound of voices. Buck Woods was standing by his pickup, talking with another man. His pickup lights were still on.

Now Buck reached inside and flicked a switch. Two powerful spotlights mounted on the cab came on. A few yards ahead was parked a smaller truck with an empty bed. Rob was to learn that the empty truck was used to transport the horses used in rounding up the cattle to be stolen.

Within the next fifteen minutes, Rob learned how the cattle rustling was carried out. It was a very efficient operation and went quickly—the results of a great deal of practice, no doubt.

About twenty head of cattle, including several calves, had been herded up against the fence of a small pasture. Two men on horseback rode herd on the bawling cattle.

The eighteen-wheeler was backed up to the makeshift corral. Rob pitched in with Buck and the man he had been talking to a few moments ago. From the bed of the eighteen-wheeler they unloaded a steel loading chute extending from the rear of the truck bed to the ground. Steel poles extended the chute, forming a sort of tunnel reaching to the fence.

Then Buck called out to the men riding herd on the cattle. He and Rob used wire cutters on the fence, snipping the four strands of wire and tying the ends to the steel poles.

Then the riders began yelling at the cattle. Bawling, pawing the dirt, the animals were squeezed into the improvised tunnel. Then they were herded up the ramp into the truck bed. They went fighting all the way, but they soon were all loaded.

After they shoved the chute into the truck and closed the gate, Rob glanced at his watch. He was astonished to notice that they had been here less than an hour. Even as the thought crossed his mind, he heard the tailgate slam shut on the other, smaller truck. Glancing over, he saw that the horses had been loaded. Now the engine fired, and the truck pulled away.

An efficient and swift operation, Rob thought.

Beside him Buck was lighting a cigarette. Apparently he guessed at Rob's thoughts. He said with a grin, "Slick as goose grease, huh, Rob?"

Rob nodded. "It's a smooth operation."

"That's the secret: in and out quick. Hardly ever takes us over an hour."

"One thing I'm wondering about," Rob said. "No matter how quiet you try to be, you must raise some noise. Especially the cattle. They carry on quite a bit."

"We never load the truck within hearing distance of any houses, and we use roads seldom used," Buck said. "The ranchers don't keep a close watch on their cattle. It would be too expensive to hire enough cowpunchers. There is always a chance of someone blundering onto us, of course, and coming close enough to hear the cattle. But it's never happened. The boss has got it all figured out to a T."

Rob wanted desperately to ask who the boss was, but that would be a stupid thing to do at this juncture. But one thing he now knew—Buck Woods wasn't the head of this criminal enterprise.

Buck added grimly, "And if anyone ever does stumble onto us, they'll wish to hell they hadn't." His hand dipped under his jacket and came up with a deadly looking automatic. Buck waved it. "I'm a good shot, and I wouldn't hesitate to use this."

Would Buck kill someone over a few head of cattle? A glance into the man's cold eyes, and Rob realized that he was fully capable of it.

Buck said, "Now it's time to get the hell out of here. You take your pickup and head out first, Rob. I'll tag along with Joy and the semi. You can go back to your motel now. I'll give you a call and meet you with your cut. We have a buyer for the beef, but it'll take a few days to cut the deal. We'll probably have another job lined up by then."

He clapped Rob on the shoulder. "Good job, buddy," he said with false geniality. "You're a good worker. But one word of warning again: keep your mouth shut."

Rob nodded. "You can depend on me."

"I know I can. Down the line we may want you to drive the eighteen-wheeler." His smile was sly. "You know women. They're not too dependable. Joy's a good driver, but she's ditzy. You drive the rig, you earn a bigger cut."

"How did you know I can drive an eighteen-wheeler?" Rob asked in surprise.

Buck's smile was a smirk. "I know that one Rob Hardesty is licensed to drive an eighteen-wheeler. I did wonder why you ain't driving one instead of working rodeos and ranches."

Rob had an answer ready. "I got tired of driving a rig. Man gets lonely out there on the highways."

"You get tired of things quick, don't you, buddy?"

Rob shrugged. "Could be."

"You better stick with this one awhile, or you may come to regret it."

"I think I'll stay around for a bit," Rob said with a grin.

"The money's better than rodeoing or training horses."

"Good!" Buck motioned. "You'd better take off now."

Buck turned away. Rob got into his pickup and drove back the way he had come. One thing had struck him as rather strange. He hadn't been introduced to the other three men, and at no time had their names been spoken aloud. He might be able to identify them if he saw them again, but not by name.

As he drove, he calculated just how much money the stolen cattle would bring. Even with today's depressed prices they should bring roughly two thousand a head. That meant that tonight's haul would come to about forty thousand dollars.

Rob whistled softly. Not bad at all for a few hours' work.

*   *   *

He didn't call Stanley Morgan until the next morning. When he got his supervisor on the phone, he told him what had happened last night.

"Hey, Rob. Good job!" Morgan said. "You say this Woods mentioned a boss?"

"Yes."

"Which means, of course, that he isn't the main honcho. No idea who he might be?"

"Not a clue, sir."

Morgan was silent for a few moments. "We could bust Woods and the rest of the crew with you last night. But that would only cut off the tail of the beast. Whoever the big guy is, he would just hire another crew and remain in business. We have to stick with it until we get a handle on the boss. You up to it, Rob?"

"Of course, sir," Rob replied. "That's what we're after, isn't it?"

"Yes. But be careful, hear?" Morgan warned. "This Buck Woods sounds like a dangerous character. He gets a sniff of your purpose, he could kill you without a second thought."

"I realize that, sir. I'll be careful. You can depend on that."

"Rob . . . One more thing. Have you learned anything that points to the killer of this man Simms? The sheriff's investigator called me yesterday. He said he's not getting anywhere with his investigation. He threatened to take you in again for questioning."

Rob sighed to himself. Another thing to worry about! He said, "I have no clue, sir. From the way Buck Woods talked about Simms, there certainly was no love lost there. Apparently Simms had a loose mouth when drinking. He may have been murdered to shut his mouth about the cattle thieves. But that's just a feeling I have. I have nothing concrete to back it up."

"Well, keep your eyes and ears open. You hear anything bearing on the murder, contact me at once." Morgan laughed lightly. "And try to keep out of Miller's way, okay?"

Rob said, "I'll do my best, sir."

*   *   *

The next few days were hard on Rob. He didn't dare do any investigating into his case. He was in the exact position that he wanted to be, but if Buck Woods got even a hint that he was sniffing around, he would blow the opportunity.

Inactivity always grated on Rob. He needed to be doing something during his waking hours. He loved to swim, but there was only so much of that he could do before he became wrinkled as a prune. Except for an occasional beer, he didn't drink, so that ruled out spending time in a bar. He liked to read, yet even that began to pall after a time.

Over the next few days he saw all the movies at the Prescott Mall theater that appealed to him. That took care of part of the day, but the only thing to do in the evenings was to watch TV. Since it was summer, rerun season, there was little of interest on the tube.

He even went to the Prescott Public Library and searched for material on cattle rustling. He had read all he could find on cattle rustling after being given the assignment. Much to his surprise there wasn't a great deal in print about the subject. Apparently it wasn't taken too seriously by law enforcement people. For that and other reasons, it made stock stealing relatively easy. According to what he had read, it was easier and more profitable than robbing a liquor store. Often the thefts were done by men who stole car radios and the like, who found an opportunity to steal a few head of cattle and did so.

Few ranchers locked their gates or checked their cattle very often. On the large ranches, with large herds, it was difficult to kept a running count. In such cases, the rancher could lose thirty or forty head and never realize it. And of course, it would be too costly to hire guards for their cattle.

That was about the extent of his knowledge. He hoped the library would have more. He did pick up a few tidbits.

The best method of stopping cattle thefts, Rob learned, was branding the animals and then registering the brands with the state. Changing brands on the cattle was too much hassle for the rustlers. If the brands were registered, potential buyers could be forewarned. This process made it too difficult for cattle rustlers.

Rob was surprised to discover that many ranchers nowadays never bothered to brand their cattle. Those who did often didn't register their brand with the state.

Rob thought back to the night he helped steal the

cattle with Buck Woods and crew. Were they branded? He was almost certain that they were, but to his chagrin he couldn't remember the brand.

But this operation was on a large scale, Rob knew. If they were sold directly to a packing-house owner with few scruples, it wouldn't matter if the cattle were branded or not. And he suspected that that was exactly what happened. As Buck had told him, the operation was well-organized. Probably right down to the moment when the steaks and roasts went on sale in the supermarkets.

Recently, cattle rustling had gone high-tech. Some took along chainsaws and butchered the cattle right on the spot. Some rigs were even refrigerated with the needed meat-processing equipment inside. The cattle could be slaughtered, loaded into the truck, and processed while the truck drove down the highway to market.

One man who had chased cattle rustlers for years wrote about it. He wrote that a hundred years ago cattle thieves would drive the cattle off on horseback. This meant that they would leave a trail behind. But with today's trucks and highways, they didn't leave much of a trail, if any.

Buck Woods and crew don't have a refrigerated truck yet, Rob thought. He wondered how long it would be before they did have one. That would make them even more difficult to catch. He hoped they would all be in jail before that happened.

Reading the literature he could find in the library on cattle rustling took Rob about an hour. Then he was at loose ends once more. So it was with both relief and surprise that he received a phone call late one afternoon. "Mr. Hardesty, this is Joy Simms."

Rob held the receiver away to stare at it in astonishment. Joy Simms was the last person he would have expected to call him. He put the receiver back to his ear and said cautiously, "Yes, Mrs. Simms?"

"Surprised, right?" She laughed slightly. "I know. But I had to be in Prescott on an errand, and I thought . . . Mr. Hardesty, would you meet me for a drink?"

Rob hesitated. What could she possibly want with him? Yet she was certainly connected to his investigation. How could anyone suspect that he was doing anything out of the way by meeting her? After all, she had contacted him. And he had to admit to feeling an enormous curiosity.

He said, "Okay, Mrs. Simms."

They agreed to meet in Murphy's Restaurant in downtown Prescott. A half hour later Rob sat across from her in a booth in the bar side of the restaurant.

Murphy's Restaurant was one of Prescott's premier attractions. The food was excellent, and the atmosphere was attractive. The building was old and had once been a country store. In converting to a restaurant, much of its charm had been retained.

Usually it was crowded, especially on weekends. But since this was a weeknight, it wasn't too busy. They could talk under the low hum of the conversation without much risk of being overheard.

Tonight Joy Simms was subdued. She wasn't drunk, and she restricted herself to two drinks, while Rob sipped at his one beer.

"I wanted to apologize to you for my behavior the last two times we met, Rob," she said, her eyes cast down. "I'd had too much to drink both times. I shouldn't have said the things I said to you."

Rob had to wonder what had changed her attitude. He said, "It was understandable. I know your husband's death had to come as a shock."

"It did, yes, but I shouldn't have taken it out on you."
Now she looked up, directly into his eyes. "I know you
didn't kill Troy."

Rob wanted to ask her how she knew that for sure, but
he refrained. "Thank you for that, Mrs. Simms."

She went on as if he hadn't spoken. "Troy and I weren't
getting along. I told you that. We didn't love each other
anymore. We stayed together as much out of habit as
anything, I suppose. But we had been husband and wife
for a long time. That has to mean something, doesn't it?"

Her eyes had the shine of tears, which surprised Rob
a little. Apparently, under all that bright lipstick and too
much makeup was a heart. He said, "Yes, it does."

She continued, "What's been upsetting me, I think, is
guilt. I feel guilty, as if I was somehow responsible for his
death. And that's silly, isn't it?"

It was clear that she was seeking sympathy, maybe
even forgiveness. Rob murmured, "I suppose we all feel
guilty when someone near us dies. Guilty that we're still
alive, and the other person isn't."

Joy didn't seem to hear him, as she stared intently down
into her drink glass. "I have to get over feeling guilt. I will
get over it. I am over it!" She gave her head a violent
shake. She looked up and beckoned to their waitress for
another drink. She smiled brightly at Rob. "There! Just
talking to you made me feel better. Thank you, Rob."

At a loss for words, Rob merely nodded. This whole
meeting didn't make a great deal of sense.

She reached out and patted his hand on the table.
"And welcome to our group, Rob. I think you'll make a
fine addition. Forget what I said the other night."

Rob seized the opportunity. He asked casually, "How
did you and your husband get involved in cattle rustling?"

"Needed the money. Same as you, I imagine," she said with a shrug. "Troy's back was bothering him a great deal. All those years driving an eighteen-wheeler overland had pounded his kidneys to mush. With this deal he didn't work the long hours, and the money was one hell of a lot better. As for me, I only drove the rig when Troy couldn't. I used to go on the road with him. He taught me how to handle the rig, so I could spell him at the wheel."

Rob took a sip of his beer. "I gather that Buck Woods isn't the boss of the crew?"

Joy laughed. "Nah. He hasn't got the brains for an operation like this."

"Who is the boss, Joy? You know?"

"No, and I don't want to know." She gave him a sharp glance. "My advice to you is, don't go nosing around asking questions like that. It's not healthy."

Rob gave a careless shrug. "No big deal. It's just that I like to know who I'm working for."

"Sometimes it's better not to know—" She broke off, looking past him.

A voice said from behind Rob, "Mrs. Simms, I'm glad to see you."

Rob looked around. A tall man with graying hair stood behind him, a drink in his hand. He looked faintly familiar.

The newcomer spoke again, "My sympathy for the loss of your husband, Mrs. Simms. A tragic thing."

Joy said, "Thank you, Mr. Babcock . . ."

Of course, Rob scolded himself, *Elmo, the clown!* It was difficult to recognize Jack Babcock without his clown makeup on.

Babcock's gaze swung around to Rob. "And . . . Mr. Hardesty, I believe?"

"Yes, Rob Hardesty." Rob stood, extending his hand. As they shook hands, he said, "You saved me from being stomped."

"Yes, of course. I remember quite well. How are you, Mr. Hardesty?"

"Fine, thank you."

Babcock glanced again at Joy. "I didn't realize you two were acquainted."

"We're just casual acquaintances, Mr. Babcock," Joy said hastily. "We just ran into each other here, and Mr. Hardesty offered to buy me a drink."

"Fine, fine!" Babcock said heartily. "Always happy to see two people enjoying themselves." With a wave of his hand Babcock turned away and walked down the bar where he took an empty stool.

Joy said hurriedly, "Thank you for the drinks, Mr. Hardesty, and for listening to me."

She picked up her purse and squirmed out of the booth, almost running in her haste to get out of the place.

Rob stared after her, puzzled. Why had she been in such a hurry to leave? And why had she made such a point of being only casually acquainted with him?

Because she was afraid that Jack Babcock would think badly of her for having a drink with a man this soon after her husband's sudden death? That was probably it, he concluded.

He left money on the table for the waitress and slid out of the booth. As he left, he looked back over his shoulder. Elmo was hunched over the bar, staring moodily down into his drink.

CHAPTER
9

It was still fairly early when Rob left the restaurant. Something had occurred to him, something he needed to check on. The only person likely to have the answer was Bill Miller. Since Miller seemed to work the night shift, he might be at the sheriff's station.

Stanley Morgan had warned him not to see the sheriff's investigator any more than was necessary. Now Rob felt that it was necessary.

Bill Miller was in. Although he didn't seem particularly pleased to see Rob, he agreed to talk to him.

Rob said, "I have a question. The body of Troy Simms. You noticed the lipstick smear on the side of his face?"

Miller gave an annoyed grunt. "This may be country to a big-city fellow like you, Hardesty . . . Whoops! Harding, isn't it? Hard to keep straight, the names of you undercover hotshots."

Rob laughed. "I'm hardly a big-city fellow, Mr. Miller."

"Whatever." Miller waved a hand. "Yes, I noticed, Harding. I'm considered a fair homicide investigator."

"Have you identified the lipstick yet?"

Miller frowned. "What do you mean, identified?"

"Who does the lipstick belong to?"

Miller grunted. "If you mean does it belong to his wife—no. At least it didn't come from any of her lipsticks. She could have tossed it, of course. But I doubt very much if the killer knows he or she left the lipstick imprint. So if Troy's wife is, by some chance, our perp, she wouldn't have had any reason to lose the lipstick."

"How do you know that the killer didn't realize the lipstick smear was left?" Rob asked.

"I don't know, Harding," Miller said shortly. "But why would the imprint be left on purpose? Unless this is a serial killer we have here, and the imprint is his mark. I don't think so." He looked thoughtful for a moment. "Of course, on second thought, he could have left it on purpose."

"Why?"

"So we cops, stupid as we are, would think the killer is a woman," Miller said in a snarling voice.

"Yes, that makes sense," Rob said with a nod.

"Well, thank you, Mr. Task Force Investigator."

Rob ignored the sarcasm. He knew how frustrating it was to be up against a blank wall in an investigation. He said, "Did Simms have a history of womanizing?"

"Not that I know about. His wife didn't know about it, nor any of his friends I've questioned. So if you're thinking it was a girlfriend who killed him, forget it. In fact . . ." His eyes turned hard as polished stones. "Why don't you forget the whole thing, Harding? I'm the homicide investigator here. You stick to cattle rustling. How is that going, by the way? Any progress?"

Rob wasn't about to share any information about his investigation with this man. He said, "Not well. I seem to be at a dead end, like you are with your homicide investigation."

Miller scowled angrily. "Let me tell you something, Harding." He tapped Rob on the chest with a blunt forefinger. "I'm not at a dead end. True, my progress isn't spectacular, but don't for an instant doubt that I'll find the killer. I'm a damned good homicide man. Sooner or later, I'll get the guy. Understand?"

Rob nodded. "Understood, sir."

"And one more thing," the sheriff's investigator continued. "If you stumble across anything, any little thing at all, bearing on the murder of Troy Simms, I'm the first to know. The very first. Is that understood?"

"Yes, sir."

"Good!" Miller waved a hand. "Then go away, and let me get back to something more important than stolen cattle."

*   *   *

Buck Woods called late the next afternoon. "Hardesty? We need to meet. I don't want to be seen visiting your motel. How about meeting in that little park off Sixth Street downtown? Fifteen minutes?"

Rob got to the park about twenty minutes later. Buck's pickup was already in the parking lot at the entrance. Buck was sitting at a picnic table, smoking. Since it was a weekday and the middle of the afternoon, the park was almost deserted. Only a woman and two small children were in the park. They were eating a picnic lunch at a table on the other side. Rob crossed to where Buck awaited him. He sat across the table from the man.

Buck took an envelope from his pocket and slid it across the table. "Here's your split."

Rob picked the envelope up without opening it and slipped it into his pocket. "Have any trouble?"

Buck tilted his head to one side, his eyes bright with suspicion. "Why should I have any trouble?"

Rob shrugged. "No reason. I just wondered."

"You wonder too much, Hardesty. It ain't healthy." Then Buck cracked a smile. "No trouble. Went smooth as butter on pancakes."

Rob ached to ask him how the sale of the stolen cattle was handled after the theft took place. But he sensed a touch of paranoia about Buck Woods. Asking the man too many questions at this stage would be unwise.

Buck leaned back, stretching with a huge yawn. "Only thing is, I've been doing some traveling these past few days. Haven't had enough sleep. Had my druthers, I'd head home and crash for a week. But I can't waste that much time." He grinned with satisfaction. "We have another job lined up. Tomorrow night. Ranch up toward Ash Fork. One advantage to that, it makes it a few less miles to drive after we load up."

Then the buyer of the cattle is located north of here, Rob thought. The destination could be located as close as Flagstaff or Kingman.

He noticed that Buck was looking at him with a crafty smile.

Buck said, "You'll be driving the eighteen-wheeler, Hardesty. Think you can handle that?"

"Sure, no problem." Belatedly, he felt a rush of excitement. This meant that he was going to learn what outfit was handling the stolen cattle on the other end. Struggling to hide his elation, he said casually,

"What's happened to Joy Simms?"

Buck gave a shrug. "Like I told you, she's flaky. She's not all that dependable. When I delivered her cut of the money to her this morning, I told her about this new deal. She said she wouldn't be driving. No reason, just that she wouldn't be going." He stared into Rob's eyes. "I'm hoping that you'll work out, Rob. If that happens, we can get rid of her. Wouldn't be too soon to suit me."

"You said that'll up my cut?"

Buck nodded. "Yep."

Rob allowed greed to show in his voice. "Then I'm all for that."

Buck laughed heartily. "Thought you would be. Well, that takes care of our business today." He stood up. "I'm going home to sleep the clock around. I'll pick you up at eight tomorrow night at your motel." With that he was gone, striding across the park toward the parking lot. Rob waited until he was out of sight, then followed. He waited until he was in his pickup before he opened the envelope and counted the money. Three thousand dollars!

He whistled softly. Not bad for three hours of his time. A thousand dollars an hour!

*   *   *

When Buck came the next night to pick Rob up, he said, "Since you're driving the eighteen-wheeler, leave your pickup here. You won't be needing it."

As they drove away, Rob said, "Have a good sleep, Buck?"

"Slept until noon today. Feel like a new man," Buck said jubilantly. "Barbara, my old lady, took the kids out early this morning and stayed out with them until this afternoon. If they'd been home, they wouldn't have let me sleep."

This was the first time that Buck had mentioned a wife and children. "How many kids do you have?" Rob asked.

"Five. A full house, two boys and three girls. Love the little rug rats." Buck laughed. "But they can be a real pain sometimes."

As they drove on, Rob had to wonder about this. It seemed odd. Here was a man with a family and apparently a happy home life. Yet, he supported them by committing criminal acts. A good family man and a thief. How could the two go together?

It wasn't the first time he'd had such thoughts since becoming an investigator. And so far he hadn't come up with any answers. Maybe there weren't any, not cut-and-dried answers, anyway.

Another thought wormed its way into his mind. Could Buck Woods also be a murderer? Had he killed Troy Simms? Again, no ready answers popped into his mind.

The Simmses eighteen-wheeler was parked in a lot behind a service station in Chino. Rob got in and started it up. The rumble of the huge diesel motor sounded like the angry roar of a movie monster. Rob studied the dashboard, trying to make sense of the many dials. Rob had worked for a time as a relief driver for an independent trucker. It had been after he left the Army and before he joined the task force. He had learned enough to qualify him for a license to operate an eighteen-wheeler. But he had never liked the job. After the newness had worn off, he had found the long hours spent on the nation's highways to be boring, not to mention butt-numbing.

He was startled out of his reverie by the passenger-side door opening. He glanced around to see Buck climbing in.

Buck settled in and closed the door. He grinned over at Rob. "I'll leave my pickup here and pick it up when we get back."

"You're riding with me?" Rob asked in surprise.

"Yep. Riding shotgun," Buck said with a laugh. Then he sobered. "You don't think I'd trust you with this rig until I'm sure you can handle it, do you, Hardesty? It's an expensive piece of machinery."

"I thought it belonged to Troy Simms."

Buck laughed again. "It did. But old Troy loved the booze too much. He got way behind with the payments, and the boss had to bail him out. The rig belongs to us now."

Rob ached to ask who "us" was but held his tongue. Instead, he said, "I can understand why you'd want to see how I handle a rig this size. I'm not all that sure myself. It's been awhile."

Buck said, "It'll probably all come back to you."

Following Buck's directions, Rob drove the semi north toward Ash Fork. He soon discovered that Buck was right—after a few miles he was comfortable with the big truck. He had it under full control.

About halfway between Chino and Ash Fork, Buck directed him to turn off onto a side road to the left. The road was gravel like the one they had driven down the other night. But it looked like it hadn't been used much of late. In the truck's powerful headlights Rob could see grass growing high between the ruts, and the road was rough and full of holes. He had to proceed slowly.

By Rob's watch it was close to eleven o'clock when Buck said suddenly, "Slow down, Hardesty. It's coming up soon now."

Rob slowed almost to a crawl. In a few moments he saw the truck he'd seen the other night parked by the side of the road. And then he saw cattle huddled on the other side of the fence, trapped in the truck's bright lights.

Buck cursed under his breath.

Rob asked, "What's wrong, Buck?"

"Look at that herd!" Buck jabbed a thumb at the cattle by the fence. "Doesn't look like much more than a dozen head! Hardly worth the trouble."

Buck was out of the cab before the truck had barely stopped rolling. He charged toward where the cattle were bunched. Rob climbed down and followed him.

By the time Rob reached the fence Buck was raging at the man standing there, the man Rob had seen the other night. "Damn it, there's not enough cattle there to spit at!"

"I'm sorry, Buck," the man said in a whining voice. "When I checked the pasture out this afternoon, there were probably thirty head gathered around here. But by the time I got out here tonight with the boys, most of them had drifted off. Nothing I could do."

"Hardly worth the trouble of loading," Buck said in a grumbling voice. But his anger had cooled now. "Well, let's get on with it."

Under Buck's directions they followed almost the same procedure as the first night. Rob maneuvered the truck, backing it up to the fence. The tailgate was removed and the chute fixed in place. The fence was cut and the wires tied to the chute gate. Then the bawling cattle were driven up the ramp and into the truck.

Again, the whole thing took less than an hour. The chute was reloaded. The others loaded their horses on the second truck. They were underway before the eighteen-wheeler was ready.

And again, Rob noticed, he was never introduced to the other three men. He had no idea of their names. Apparently Buck wanted it that way.

In the truck cab Buck motioned. "Let's move it, get

this over with! The boss ain't going to be too happy about the haul tonight."

The burning question was, who was the boss? It was becoming clear to Rob that Buck was the only person in the entire operation who actually knew the identity of the head man. Rob gritted his teeth and kept quiet.

As they approached the highway, Buck said, "Turn north. We're heading to Kingman."

This time Rob had been careful to check to see if the stolen cattle wore brands. They were branded—JK. He said, "The cattle back there are branded. Won't that cause a problem getting rid of them? What if the owner has registered the brand with the state?"

"Won't matter. That's all been taken into consideration," Buck said with a smug grin. "As I told you before, the boss has everything covered. The slaughterhouse owner in Kingman couldn't care less about brands. The cattle back there become steaks and roasts for the table not too long after he takes them off our hands."

*   *   *

It was shortly after sunrise when they reached Kingman. Kingman was in the heart of cattle country.

As they entered the outskirts of town, Buck said, "The place won't be open for a couple of hours yet. Get off the freeway at the next exit and we'll have breakfast."

Rob obeyed the instructions, pulling the big rig off the highway. He could handle the truck expertly now. The freeway exit ramp led into a truck stop open twenty-four hours a day. Highway 40 was well-traveled with trucks hauling freight across the country. The lot surrounding the service station and restaurant was packed with eighteen-wheelers. Signs indicated that the restaurant provided showers and similar facilities for truck drivers only.

As they got out of the truck cab, Buck said, "You go on in, Hardesty, and get us a booth. I'll be in in about ten minutes. I have a phone call to make."

Buck headed toward a line of pay phones against one wall. Rob would have loved to have eavesdropped on the call Buck was about to make; he felt confident that the call was to the mysterious "boss."

He went on into the restaurant and found an empty booth. He ordered a cup of coffee from the waitress when she came. "There's someone with me," he said. "He'll be in in a few minutes."

Buck's mood was dark when he came into the restaurant. He slid into the booth and snatched up the menu, scowling as he read it. Rob judged that it wouldn't be a good idea to inquire as to what had disturbed him.

When their food was served, they ate mostly in silence. Only idle remarks passed between them. Buck killed time after they finished eating, drinking three more cups of coffee. Finally he shoved his empty cup back and said, "Okay, let's hit the road. Kane's should be open about now."

Buck directed Rob to drive to an industrial area on the edge of town. The area was a hodgepodge of dreary looking buildings. The buildings were low, square structures, all the same color. They looked like scattered children's building blocks. Rob could smell the odor of slaughtered animals well before they reached the building. There was a sign in front: Kane's Meats.

Buck told him to drive around back. There was a loading dock. Rob backed the semi up to the dock. Just as he got the truck bed against the dock, overhead doors on the building side of the dock rolled up, and several men emerged.

As Rob and Buck approached the dock, one of the men spoke. "Hello, Buck. Load looks a little light today."

The man was short, in his fifties, with a moon face. He looked greasy, like he'd been around slaughtered animals so long that he now wore a permanent coating of lard.

"Tell me about it," Buck said in a growling voice. "Let's get on with it, Kane." Buck hoisted himself onto the dock. He looked down at Rob. "You stay here. Keep an eye out. These guys'll steal your teeth if you don't watch them like a hawk."

The man named Kane cackled with laughter, draped an arm around Buck's shoulders, and led him into the building. Again, Rob noted, he hadn't been introduced.

The other men on the dock hauled out high boards and attached them to the back of the truck bed and to the building door. This formed a rough chute. While Rob watched, the tailgate was removed. Cattle prods were brought out and rammed through the slats in the sides of the truck bed.

Bawling and rattling the boards, the cattle were herded inside the building. Then the makeshift chute was taken apart and carried back inside. It was only a few minutes later when Buck returned. He nodded to Rob without speaking and jumped to the ground, heading toward the truck cab.

Rob got in and started the motor. As they drove away from the building, he said, "They unload pretty fast. One thing surprised me. I thought they'd unload the cattle into holding pens, not right into the building."

Buck grunted. "Yeah. Wouldn't surprise me if most of the cattle aren't already slaughtered and on the assembly line by this time. Kane is an old hand at this. When stolen cattle are brought in, especially a small batch like we had today, they're dispatched right to cattle heaven. Less chance of being caught out that way."

Rob let a note of admiration show in his voice.

"They've got it down to a science."

Buck grunted again. "Yeah. But the boss ain't going to be happy. Picked up less than fifteen grand today." He patted his pocket. "At least you can get your cut today without delay."

"You mean, he paid in cash?" Rob said in surprise.

Buck laughed harshly. "You think he'd pay by check in a deal like this? No way. Probably won't be seeing Kane for awhile. I talked to the boss on the phone back there. We decided something."

"Decided what?" Rob asked.

"We're going to steal mostly horses for awhile. Cattle just ain't paying off too well right now. In fact . . ." Buck turned a mocking grin on Rob. "We decided that the first place we'll hit will be Jonas Greene's place. That should give you a boost, getting back at old Jonas for firing you, Hardesty."

CHAPTER 10

Stunned, Rob drove for a few miles in silence.

Finally Buck chuckled. "What? Nothing to say, Hardesty? I thought you'd be hooting with glee."

Rob gave a small start and glanced over to meet Buck's taunting gaze. He said, "Oh, I'd like to see Jonas Greene get his. But I was just thinking about it. Isn't stealing his horses going to present problems?"

Buck shrugged. "Such as?"

"It's not like the cattle. They've all been miles from the ranch headquarters. But Greene's horses are all located in the pasture close by. None of the horses are more than a mile from the ranch house. How can you get them without Jonas hearing? He's got a couple of shotguns, and he'll use them, believe me."

"Easy enough. The boss and I talked about that briefly,"

Buck said. "We lure Greene, the whole family, away from home."

"And just how are you going to manage that?"

"We haven't figured that out yet," Buck replied. "But it'll come. Maybe you can dream up something." Buck hit him lightly on the shoulder. "You strike me as a good idea man."

Rob gave a derisive snort. "Yeah, right. I'll think about it, but don't hold your breath."

*   *   *

It was past noon when they got back to the lot where the eighteen-wheeler had been parked. Rob shut everything down, locked the cab, and crossed to where Buck was waiting in his pickup. He gave Buck the keys to the semi.

Buck drove toward Prescott. They rode most of the way in silence. Rob's thoughts were on Jonas Greene. He wasn't thinking of ways to get the family off the ranch; his hope was that Buck or the "boss" wouldn't come up with a scheme that would work.

How could he help steal Greene's horses? The rancher had been kind to him, and Rob liked all three Greenes. If he helped steal the horses and Alan ever found out about it, his sense of betrayal would be painful. It might destroy his faith in mankind for the rest of his life.

No, Rob didn't want to participate in the theft of the horses. Yet, how could he refuse? Even if he could dream up a reason to back out, he would certainly arouse Buck's suspicions, and he would probably be thrown out of the rustling gang. That might not even be the worst of it— they might try to kill him.

If he backed out now, all of his work would have gone for nothing. He felt that he was getting very close to learning the identity of the ringleader of the rustlers.

Buck pulled his pickup up in front of the motel,

interrupting Rob's thoughts. Buck reached into his pocket and took out a roll of bills. He stripped off six hundred-dollar bills and gave them to Rob.

"Sorry it's not more, Hardesty. If we steal Greene's nags, your cut will be much larger. Bet on it."

"That's okay," Rob said absently, his thoughts on other things. He got out of the pickup and waved as Buck drove off with a screech of tires.

Instead of going immediately to his room, Rob walked a block up the street to a diner. He ordered a sandwich and a cold drink. He nibbled on the sandwich when it came. He was still troubled over what to do about Jonas and the horses.

A half hour later, he was talking to Stanley Morgan from a pay phone just outside the cafe. Rob finished telling his supervisor about the cattle rustling and Buck's plans for stealing the horses. Morgan said, "At least we have one puzzle cleared up. When we crack down on this crew of rustlers, we'll know who to nail on the sales end. Good job, Rob." Morgan paused for a few moments, then said, "But why do I get the feeling that something's troubling you?"

"It's Greene's horses, sir," Rob said. "Knowing in advance and not warning him. Jonas Greene is skating on the edge. If he loses his horses, he probably faces bankruptcy."

Morgan said, "You've been in on the theft of two herds of cattle, Rob. Do you feel bad about those ranchers?"

"Yes, I do," Rob replied. "But it's not the same thing. I don't know them. I know Jonas and his family, and I like them. I'd hate to be responsible for Jonas losing his ranch."

"I'm sure he has insurance covering any stock losses."

"I'm not so sure," Rob said. "He never told me so directly, but I suspect he doesn't have insurance. Jonas is not a great businessman."

"Rob, that's good of you to feel concern, but you're an undercover investigator." Morgan's voice held a note of exasperation. "What would you rather do? Warn him, so he could save his horses? Or keep your mouth shut and catch our stock thieves? This may be the one, the one where you learn who's ramrodding this crew. We have to balance the loss of Greene's animals against other ranchers losing their stock in the future. Or maybe . . ." Here, Morgan's voice took on a note of sarcasm. "Or maybe you think the task force should reimburse Greene for any losses? Is that it, Rob?"

Rob was silent.

"Well, for your information, the task force doesn't have that kind of budget. Look at it this way, Rob. If we catch these thieves soon enough, maybe we can seize enough assets to repay some, if not all, of the rancher's losses." Morgan's voice had returned to normal. "I appreciate your position, Rob. But as an investigator, there'll be times when you have to make hard choices. This is one of them. A veteran cop once told me that a cop should never get personally involved with the victim of a crime. It tends to warp the cop's judgment. You'd do well to remember that, Rob."

"That's easy enough to say," Rob said with a sigh. "But it's much harder in practice."

"Perhaps." Morgan's voice hardened again. "But that's the way it has to be."

The supervisor banged down the phone without saying good-bye. Rob realized that Stanley Morgan was displeased with him. Rob hung up slowly. This was the first time during their association that Morgan had been angry with him. But Morgan's displeasure didn't stop Rob from worrying about Jonas Greene.

The problem nagged at him for the rest of the day. He

spent some time in the pool, but while his body was engaged, his mind was in a turmoil. If was almost as if his mind was detached from his body. He imagined his spirit hovering over the pool, gazing down at him while he swam.

He ate dinner that evening with little appetite. For the first time in his life, he was tempted to walk to the bar up the street and get drunk. Maybe that would blank out his thoughts for a while.

He resisted the temptation and returned to the motel. He found a movie on an old movie channel that snagged his attention—*The Greatest Show on Earth*. He had seen the movie before, but this time he got caught up in all the excitement and color. The performance of Charlton Heston as the man running the circus was great. And Jimmy Stewart, as the sad clown, was very touching. It was a satisfying movie, and Rob went to bed in a better mood. The movie was still on his mind as he drifted off to sleep.

He awoke with a start some time later, sitting up in bed, fully alert. He knew who Buck's "boss" was! It had all come together in his mind. But the problem was he had absolutely no evidence. There was nothing that he could take to Stanley Morgan or the police.

He lay back down with little thought of sleep, his mind busy. There had to be a way to nail the guilty person. If he talked to Morgan, the supervisor might have some suggestions, but Rob knew that he wouldn't do that. If he were to reveal the leader of the cattle rustlers and save Greene's horses at the same time, he had to do it on his own.

He lay awake for hours, his plan gradually taking shape in his mind.

*   *   *

The next day, Rob made four phone calls. The first one was to Buck Woods.

"Hey, Hardesty!" Buck said. "What's up, buddy?"

"You asked me to try and think of a way to lure Greene and his family away from his place while we stole his horses? Well, I thought of a way."

"You did?" Buck said with a laugh. "I told the boss that you were one smart cookie. What is it? We sure as hell haven't been able to come up with anything."

"Well, I'd rather wait to tell you what it is," Rob said. "Maybe my idea won't work. If I don't tell you now, then I won't have egg on my face."

Buck's response came slowly. "Well, okay." He laughed suddenly. "What the hey! So long as it works."

"There is one thing. If my idea draws the Greenes away from their place, it'll have to be tonight. Only way it'll work. Can you have everything ready by then?"

"Sure, Hardesty. No problem. Never takes us long to hitch up the wagons and move."

"Stick to the phone, Buck," Rob said. "If all goes well, I'll call you later today with the word."

"Will do, buddy," Buck said cheerfully. "I figured a chance to get back at Jonas Greene would light a fire under your tail."

Yeah, right, Buck, Rob thought as he hung up.

During the next hour, he made three more calls. The first two required considerable persuasion to get his point across. The third was quick and short, brutally short. Rob was unsure if his brief message would work. This call was crucial to his plan; if it didn't work, the plan would fail.

He hesitated, still in the phone booth. He even picked up the receiver again and started to punch out his supervisor's number. No! He hung up the receiver. Not only would Stanley Morgan not approve of his plan, he would be very angry. But if Rob succeeded . . .

Rob thought of the old saying: Nothing succeeds like success.

Of course, if he failed, he would likely lose his job with the task force. Well, he could always return to rodeoing.

Yeah, sure! He laughed wryly to himself and returned to the motel.

*   *   *

That evening at nine o'clock, Rob drove up to the Greene Ranch in his pickup. The ranch house was dark. He drove on past the main house toward the horse corrals. The eighteen-wheeler was already there. So was Buck's pickup, and the smaller truck used to transport the rustler's horses. The men Rob had never been introduced to were unloading the horses from the truck.

In the lights of his pickup Rob saw Buck standing by the semi in conversation with Joy Simms. Rob had called earlier in the day to give Buck the go-ahead for tonight. At this time, Buck had told him that Joy wanted to drive for tonight. He added that this would be the last job on which she would be driving the eighteen-wheeler.

This was fine with Rob since it would end right here, tonight, one way or the other.

He got out of his pickup and walked over to the pair.

Buck said, "Well, here's the genius! Now, you promised to tell me how you managed to get the Greenes away from here. I can't wait to hear."

"It was simple really," Rob said with a shrug. "I'd learned that the only relative that Greene has is a brother down in Texas. His son is quite fond of his uncle. I called them and pretended to be associated with a Dallas hospital. I told

Jonas that Mark Greene had been admitted with a severe heart attack."

Buck stared. "And that's all it took?"

"That's all," Rob replied. "Like I said, they're all quite fond of Jonas's brother. I waited up at the highway. They came racing out about an hour after I called. I followed them to the Prescott airport. They caught a commuter flight into Sky Harbor Airport in Phoenix. Then I called you to tell you it was on for tonight."

Buck shook his head admiringly. "I'll be damned! Well, whatever. It worked." He glanced toward the truck being unloaded. "The guys are finished with unloading the horses. Why don't you hop over and get one of the horses, help them round up the horses in the pastures . . ."

"No, Buck," said a voice softly behind them. "You go tell them to get started. I want Mr. Hardesty here."

Rob turned slowly. A man stood in the shadow of the truck bed. But there was just enough light to cast a beam off the pistol in his hand, pointing at Rob. The man moved a single step, and his face came into the light. It was Jack Babcock—Elmo the clown without the makeup. There was nothing clownish about him at the moment. His face was cold and deadly.

A gasp came from Buck. "What are you doing here?"

"I also got a phone call. I was told that unless I made an appearance here tonight, my whole operation would be blown. But never mind, Buck . . ." Babcock motioned with the gun. "Do what I told you."

Buck went toward the truck, still looking back over his shoulder.

When he was out of hearing Babcock said, "I assume you made the call, Hardesty?"

Rob noticed Joy Simms off to one side, listening avidly. If

Babcock was aware of her presence, he paid her no heed.

Rob said, "Yes, I made the call."

"You're undercover, right?" Babcock asked. "Working for what agency?"

Rob knew that it didn't matter now. "Yes, I'm working with the Governor's Task Force on Crime. I'm investigating the stock rustling up here."

Babcock made a face. "That outfit. What put you onto me?"

Rob said, "A couple of things. First, everything I heard about you pointed to you being broke, hurting for money. Yet, at that rodeo benefit the other day, I saw you donate a thousand bucks. If you were destitute, how could you do that?"

Babcock grunted. "A stupid mistake. A man just has to show off now and again, though." His grin was mocking. "Or maybe I was just in a charitable mood at the time."

"And then there was the murder of Troy Simms." Out of the corner of his eye Rob saw Joy grow tense. "You shot him, didn't you?"

Babcock's hand tightened around the gun in his hand. "Pretty sharp, aren't you, Hardesty?" Then he shrugged. "But what does it matter now? You're never going to tell anyone. Yeah, I killed the sucker. How did you get onto me?"

"The imprint of lipstick on his cheek." Rob smiled tightly. "I was watching a movie, saw Jimmy Stewart playing a clown, and it came to me just like that. Why did you plant the kiss on his cheek? Did you want the police to think a woman had killed him?"

Babcock shrugged. "That thought crossed my mind, yeah. But mainly I thought that a kiss of death was fitting. Troy had a loose mouth. His reaction when you mentioned rustlers tipped you off, didn't it?"

"It started me thinking that he was hooked in somehow, yes," Rob said with a nod. "But why tie the body to a horse and leave him at my trailer? As a warning to me to lay off?"

Babcock shook his head. "I didn't know you were investigating my business. If I had, I would have taken you out then or had it done. No, after your fight with Troy and his threat to kill you, I thought maybe the cops would nail you for his murder." He smiled coldly. "It almost worked. I suppose it didn't because they found out you were a damned cop!"

"'Investigating your business,' you said. Do you consider stealing stock a business, a legitimate business, Babcock?" Rob asked.

Babcock's color rose, and for the first time he showed some animation. An old bitterness burned in his flat eyes. "Yes, it's my business. As for legitimate, I've been legitimate all my life, up until I started this. And where did being legitimate get me? I've never made any real money following rodeos, and now I'm getting too old and broken-down to even do that. My wife left me several years ago, taking most of my money. I was reduced to living in a house trailer." His face worked. "I got sick and tired of being broke. I decided to start stealing stock. It's easy for me, knowing all the ranchers and their spreads . . ."

"And who would suspect a clown, right?" Rob said. He lowered his face until his mouth was directly over the microphone taped to his chest. He muttered, "You got enough, Miller?"

He glanced up in time to see Babcock go rigid, glaring. "Who are you talking to? Are you wearing a wire?"

Rob saw Babcock's finger begin to tighten on the trigger of the pistol. He heard Miller's voice through the receiver in his ear: "Yes, Harding. Enough. We're coming in!"

Rob heard the sound of a shot, and he tensed for the

impact of the bullet. Yet he felt nothing. He saw Babcock half-turn toward Joy, a look of utter astonishment on his face. And then Rob realized that she held a gun in her hand. It was pointed at Babcock, a wisp of smoke coming from the barrel.

"You murdered Troy," she said in a trembling voice. "You killed my husband!"

Jack Babcock was falling slowly, falling in on himself. He fell face down in the dirt and lay still. Rob moved warily to Joy. She offered no resistance as he took the gun from her hand.

She looked at him emptily. "He killed Troy."

"I know, Joy. It's okay, just take it easy," he said.

Even as he spoke, he could hear sirens approaching. He saw spinning red lights painting the sky like lightning flashes. Bill Miller and his men had been parked only a short distance away.

*   *   *

An hour later Bill Miller came over to where Rob sat in his pickup with the door open. Rob felt weary and drained from the sudden violence of this night. Buck and the other men had been arrested and taken away. An almost catatonic Joy had also been taken away, and Babcock's body had been picked up by an ambulance.

Miller said, "I think we can just about write closure on this one. You did a good job, Harding. You're a good investigator. I still think you took a hell of a risk here. If not for Joy Simms, you could be dead right now."

"I know," Rob said in a tired voice. "But this was the only way I could see to do it." He smiled slightly. "As my supervisor might say, whatever works. What's going to happen to Joy?"

Miller shrugged. "I don't know. It's out out of my hands. Somebody higher up will have to make the final decision. My guess is they'll rule it self-defense. Even if they charge her, a good attorney will probably plead temporary insanity and get her off."

"I hope they don't charge her," Rob said. "She did save my life."

"Yeah," Miller said with a nod. "I'll need a statement from you, Harding. But the morning will be fine."

"No problem," Rob said.

"I'm not sure if it's been a pleasure, but thanks, Harding."

Miller stuck out his hand, and Rob shook it.

Miller said, "You sticking around?"

"I'm waiting for the Greenes," Rob said. He heard the sound of a vehicle approaching. "That's probably them now."

With a nod Miller got into his car and drove down the long driveway, meeting the Greene pickup on the way. Rob stood waiting until the pickup stopped beside his. Jonas Greene got out, and Marge and Alan emerged from the passenger side.

Jonas said, "Is it all over, Rob?"

"It's all over." Rob quickly told them what had taken place here tonight.

Jonas shook his head in wonder. "Elmo a cattle thief and a murderer? Who would ever have thought it? I never did care much for Jack Babcock, but a killer? Hard to believe."

"I found it hard to believe also," Rob said "I suppose that's why it took me so long to figure it all out."

"Rob . . ." Jonas hesitated in embarrassment. "I'm sorry for booting you off the ranch the way I did. But, you know, Alan—"

Rob interrupted him, "No need to apologize, Jonas. I understand."

Alan approached shyly. He tugged at Rob's sleeve, his face upturned. "I never did believe you was a bad man, Rob!"

"*Were*, Alan, not *was*," Marge said. "I was never fully convinced, either, Rob—for what it's worth."

Rob said, "It's worth a great deal, Marge. Thanks."

"The boy did believe in you, Rob," Jonas said. "In fact, I don't think I would have tumbled us all into the pickup and off the property after your call, but for him. At first I thought it was you behind everything, getting rid of me to steal my stock. But Alan finally convinced me otherwise."

"Well, now." Rob gazed down into the boy's upturned face, feeling some embarrassment of his own. "Thanks for the faith, buddy."

"Rob, can you stay and teach me how to ride now?" Alan asked eagerly.

Rob laughed and squatted on his heels, his face on a level with the boy's. "I might be able to stick around for a couple of weeks and see what we can do about that. If it's all right with your folks."

"It's all right with us," Jonas and Marge said in unison.

Rob placed a hand on the boy's shoulder. "It's settled then. If you promise to do just what I say."

Alan clapped his hands. "I promise," he said happily. "I promise, Rob!"

"That'll be the day!" Jonas said.

And then they were all laughing together happily.